Forbidden Love

By Susan Hatton

Copyright © Susan Hatton 2014

The author or authors assert their moral right under the Copyright, Designs and Patents Act, 1988, to be identified as the author or authors of this work.

All Rights reserved. No part of this publication may be reproduced, copied, stored in a retrieval system, or transmitted, in any form or by any means, without the prior written consent of the author or publisher, nor be otherwise circulated in any form of binding or cover other than that in which it is published and without a similar condition being imposed on the subsequent purchaser.

Forbidden Love

Susan Hatton

Forbidden Love

Chapter one.

Demetre sits hiding in the tree branches for hours every evening, waiting for the group of teenagers at their *spot* on the beach. The sky is so clear it gives him a perfect view of the stars twinkling, scattered over a blanket of darkness like diamonds and stretching as far as the eye can see to wrap around the edge of the world as though holding it within a lovers embrace. It contrasts so strongly with the violent rage of the ocean as it pounds against the cliff edge with enough intensity to eventually wear away the surface. Nature is letting the might of its force be known tonight, and it makes the perfect environment in which to lose one's self in thought, dreaming of things that can never truly be.
He shifts on the tree branch as he finds a more comfortable position, twigs sticking out at awkward angles making the task a difficult one to do in silence. This was what kept him going through his agonisingly eventless days, the only thing he had to look forward to anymore. The joy of knowing he could retreat to this spot while the weather was so humid, and the humans would be along come night fall to play and frolic in the frosty waters was his only escape from real life and the torture that awaited at home. The humans with their carefree games and frivolous antics being the only excitement to his otherwise mundane existence.

With the harsh crashing of waves below him and the serene view of the stars above for company he quickly loses himself within his own whirring mind, trying desperately to make a little bit of sense from his strange and exhausting day. When he left his room that morning he was instantly confronted by his insane mother who ever so politely informed him that he is now engaged, and that his bride to be will be making an appearance in the next few days in order for the preparations to begin.

She reminded him of his need to wed before his nineteenth birthday which was in just over three weeks' time, and she also informed him that his ridiculous obsession with love is outdated and it was time for him to grow up and accept his place in society. He must marry Essy Valentine and keep the family honour which his father; Dracula himself, had worked so hard to achieve.

As he tried desperately to tell her yet again of his dreams of finding a soul mate, how he felt the weight of the world on his shoulders until he escaped to the beach every night to watch the carefree humans. She had held up her hand to silence him as though he were a mere slave and told him to drop the idea of love. "Love does not exist Demetre, and it is time you stopped fantasising about it. We are the family of Dracula, we have an image to uphold and there are expectations we must meet. Do you wish to see me with nothing? A beggar hiding in the bushes all day from the vile sun as I have no shelter nor food?" she loved to try the guilt trip on him.

"Of course not mother, I intend only to find happiness. Isn't that what you want for me?" he had asked, the thoughts running through his mind that surely his mother, the woman who carried him and nurtured him within her should want her only son to meet the girl of his dreams and fall passionately and hopelessly in love before making her his bride and whisking her off for their happily ever after. But that isn't the case.

"Darling." She had replied, her hand stroking his face as though being protective although the action comes across more manipulative. "Love is not for us. We have no goddess, we have no mother, and we have no love nor kindness. We just... are. Our kind are left to wither in the shadows and do what we can to survive. And for us, that means you marrying Essy Valentine."

Demetre had truly looked at his mother in that moment, as he realised she was telling him to give up on all hope of ever finding happiness with love and to do as he was told. He saw the brown eyes encased in red eye shadow, the dark red lips to match the corset of her dress, he saw the way she wore her best clothes at eight in the morning or eight in the evening and the truth of how shallow she was had hit him like a tonne of bricks. She wore as much red as possible to give the impression she had Dracula's power, she wanted to intimidate others and be seen as a threat.

This woman had no emotional attachment to her child, she just hoped to marry him off to the highest bidder so that she might keep buying those dam expensive corsets he hated so much. Why must a woman wear something that looks so good but causes so much distress? They force a woman's bust to look bigger and her waist to look smaller as though that design is natural. He much preferred that if a woman was skinny she accepted it or if she was curvy she accepted that. All women can be beautiful without forcing their bodies into these torture devices.

"But mother that isn't to survive, that is to keep us where we are in society. I can't help but think you have sold my happiness to the highest bidder. Why I bet the twins won't be married off by their nineteenth birthdays, father would never allow it! If he discovered you were organising weddings for THEM with men they had never met he would have your throat out!"

"You want to burden your sisters with this?" she had recoiled in shock as though HE was the unreasonable one!

"No mother, I wish for you to tell me why it is acceptable to do this to me and yet unthinkable that this should be done to them. Why can I not find love in my own time? Why can you not stand proud and state your son will marry this Essy *if* we do indeed love each other? Why is my future in your hands?"

"Oh Demetre, that is enough childishness. Come down for breakfast, your duties will need to be started soon if you wish to be done for supper time." She snapped and turned, walking briskly away signalling the end of the conversation. Demetre knew that by duties she meant being seen with her in front of people. Which meant they would be entertaining again.

Some of the nearby vampire families would stop in now and then to say hello and catch up with some gossip. For some reason Driana, his mother, had always insisted on them being well dressed so as to parade them around. She was extremely eager for them to join in with as much conversation as they could muster as a way of showing off their highly expensive education. It had been a shock when the twins, Brianna and Immara, started to find their true identities. One would constantly 'accidentally' let slip what their mother had been saying about people behind their backs while the other would stick her elbow out to jab her sister and say "That was supposed to be a secret." The part which always made Demetre laugh was that it changed which twin was which personality, meaning that they planned the whole thing, which was pretty cool to say they were seven.

"You two are going to be capable of great things." He had told them one night whilst tucking them in.

"We know." They had both replied at the same time.

Demetre had followed Driana in a complete daze thinking of the twins and how much he missed them while they were away at school. With parents like theirs he know it would be his job to care for them but he hadn't known just how much he would love them. He watched his feet move one in front of the other until he had found himself seated at the table with a plate of eggs and toast in front of him, and that started another day of parties and wine and pretending to be interested in the rubbish spouting from his mother's mouth.

The echo of the sound he makes bouncing off the cliff edge as he chuckles sarcastically out loud reminds him what he is doing, and he instantly looks around to make sure there is no one that could have heard him. Angry with himself for almost blowing his cover already he hears voices around the cliffs edge, alerting him that the humans would be making an appearance momentarily. He shuffles back slightly to hide himself more within the shadows surrounding him and watches patiently for the entertainment to begin.

This few hours every evening; hidden within the branches of this tree, are the nearest to freedom he experiences in his lonely existence. Watching as they dive and splash in the water he can almost pretend to be part of them. He tried once, but questions arise when the humans start to realise he dives much deeper, jumps much higher, swims much faster, and can hold his breath for much longer than they can. Yes, even swimming with them is a bad idea. Questions mean they are getting curious, and if they find out who he is they will never let his family stay here.

The sounds become louder as the group of teenagers turn the corner into their little area, hidden from view of the rest of the beach. They put down their bags and begin removing their clothes as always ready to plunge into the icy depths awaiting them. Demetre sits on his branch above the clearing, he could sit more comfortably down there where the branches merge with the water but the humans like to use that secluded clearing for privacy sometimes. That's where two of them will sneak off and *make out* as it is called. The group of adolescents open beer bottles and light cigarettes with smiles reaching from ear to ear, no music box with them tonight so they are left with the sounds of their own voices as they forget their troubles in life for a short time.

"Hey Ashley save me some on that sugar." One of the males yell over to the girl holding the cigarette.

"Sorry scot but Nadia already asked me, you'll have to get your own." She replies and puts the cigarette in her mouth as her hands reach down to lift her top over her stomach.

He had seen many breasts in his almost nineteen years so when she managed to remove one arm and take the cig out of her mouth and pull the top over her head the sight did not even cause him to stir. It was the look in one of the other male's eyes that had him leaning forward slightly.

This Ashley girl had no problem with taking her clothes off in public and in all honesty Demetre couldn't blame her. She was beautiful. Not exactly his type but credit where credit was due, she had curves in all the right places. Her hips where definatly built for child bearing and her breasts were a healthy size and not in the slightest bit droopy. Which although these things made not a dam bit of difference to a woman's personality nor her ability to be a good wife or mother, he understood these are things women are these days obsessed with about themselves.

But the look in this boys eyes was not hunger for her body, it was not leery or creepy at all. This boy admired her. The passion for her written all over his face as he watched her confidently remove her clothes, pass the cigarette to her friend and step into the water. He quickly stripped himself of all clothing and followed her into the ice cold water. Demetre watched with new interest as this boy lingered around her and made his attempts to grab her attention, transfixed by the fact that what he was watching right now was not a mere crush, but infatuation. This boy looked ready to swim to the ends of the world for her should she wish. He also seemed terribly shy, as though his courageous exterior was just a show, a pretence. After a few beers however he seems to grow in confidence, splashing her and dunking her where shortly before he daren't get near her in case he touched her and offended her, watched with eyes that burned as the other males got too close or gestured jokingly to her exposed breasts. This man was ready to protect her, and that had Demetres attention glued to them. He dreamed of finding love and this may be the closest he ever gets if his mother gets her way.

Eventually the male manages to get Ashley alone and corners her, as she smiles and backs away playfully.

"Hey Ashley." He says with his voice turned into a sexy growl Demetre knew meant he was turned on.

"Hi Scot. Is everything alright?" she purred in response, alerting Scot, and unknown to her Demetre too, that she too is very much interested in Scot! The triumphant gleam in Scots eyes showing Demetre he too had picked up on the tone in her voice.

"Yeah, but they could be better. There's a party this weekend and I have no one to take." He swims closer to her as she tilts one side of her mouth in a knowing smile. Pretending she has no interest in him or what he is talking about but all the way her seductive lips are giving the game away. The way she pouts at him when she talks, and the way she can't seem to shake the smile from her face. The entire time they talk her eyes are practically begging for him to come closer.

"Oh, well I think Anna's free. Or I could ask Nadia for you?" She smirks, mocking him. He laughs and swims right up to her, making her smile vanish and her breathing increase as their eyes lock.

"But I don't want to take Anna." He whispers into her ear after leaning so close his head almost sits on her shoulder. She closes her eyes and tilts her head back slightly as she feels the sensation of his warm breath against the skin on her neck, nipples hardening as they peak out an inch above the surface of the water.

"Who *do* you want to take?" she asks with her voice shaking slightly, eyes still closed and arm going round to rest on his shoulder and hang loosely at his back, fingertips lightly stroking the flesh of his spine as his skin seems to shudder at the touch.

"You." He kisses her neck and she moans softly. He pulls up from her and turns around, the others are in sight but haven't noticed them. He pulls her behind him and she follows, giggling, and they make their way into the hidden clearance directly below Demetre.

Scot pushes Ashley gently against a tree branch that is half submerged in the water, it is curved at the perfect height for her to perch her bottom on to sit and lean her back against it, her breasts still exposed above the water. Scot moves in and presses his body against hers as their lips crash together, her hands reaching up to bury themselves in his hair as his hands disappear under the water to seemingly rest upon her hips. Demetre turns his head slightly for a better view as he feels something stirring within him.

The sound of moaning from below sounds like it is coming from both of them as their body's rock against each other, rubbing and thrusting and god only knows what else! Scots hands are around her back when she pulls away and starts kissing and nibbling at his chest, he brings one hand round to her front which remains under the water as the other comes round to play with her nipple. She moans as his arm is moving slightly and it's obvious to Demetre he is exploring her under the privacy of the ripples. Demetre wonders why he is so excited watching this for a moment before realising these two humans need each other. It is not the sex that is so intriguing, it is the passion in which they desire each other that has him sitting in the tree branches watching them with his own erection threatening to tear through his jeans.

When her hand disappears below the water to his front; clearly exploring him in return, and starts to move slightly Demetre imagines her hand caressing the length of him with the same need in her eyes she has for this man, and he almost starts moaning himself! This is exactly what he wants, that kind of animal attraction that leaves everybody around you wanting more and more let alone those two. The sexual tension is exhilarating as he watches scot move slowly in towards her and her head tilt all the way back, mouth forming the shape of an O with eyes closed so tightly she must be fighting off the screams of pleasure.

A choking sound almost escapes his throat as it becomes clear to Demetre that they are making love. The "Oh" sound coming from her mirroring the "Mm" sound coming from him no louder than murmurs of lust as their bodies meet, making it very obvious that he is entering her under the water, his arms wrap protectively around her waist and look as though to hold her backside as he starts to rock his pelvis. Her ankles appear out of the water and cross around his waist. Her arms snake around to his shoulders as she finds his mouth with hers.

Lust erupts within the small enclosure of branches. Demetres breathing becomes more rapid as he watches, entranced by the effect love and lust can have on two people. Of course he had experienced sex before, even sat back and watched it in his years. But this is pure lust, one hundred percent animalistic need and urgency mingled together in the great game of love making.

"Oh Scott." Says Ashley breathlessly as he lovingly replies "Yes Ashley, yes!" and thrusts harder and faster through the water as she moans and whispers his name, trying her best not to let the others hear them. His thrusts become harsh, and after a few more seconds he slams his body against hers, breathing her name and holding her tight against him as she strokes the back of his neck with her fingers.

This is where Demetre first noticed the other set of eyes in the clearing, only these eyes were *under* the water.

Demetres breath caught as he noticed the red eyes in the water were also watching the couple, and they did not look threatening in the slightest. Instead they looked... Beautiful? A pair of red eyes surrounded by strange green water, and he found himself attracted to them? As he leaned ever so slightly closer a branch snapped, the couple didn't even flinch until the loud splash had them both covering their eyes from the sprayed water. They looked completely freaked out as Scot moved Ashley behind him, looking all around for danger. The others diving into the cove to see what all the noise was.

"Hey we wondered where you guys snuck of to." Says one in a mock offensive tone raising his eye brows suggestively.

"I think it's time we left." Says Scot as he holds Ashley's hand and leads her away from the cove, with the others following behind. They quickly gather their clothes and keep walking down the beach.

Chapter 2.

Demetre tore his attention from the group of teenagers walking quickly away from the grove on the beach, struggling to get their clothes back on while rushing away, and the same splashing sound that had frightened them off moments before was heard directly below him. When he turned to investigate he saw the exact same pair of magnificent red eyes in the water returning for a closer look.

A night creature is noticed by the red in their eyes, in Demetres eyes he had a perfect red ring around the pupils. This meant he came from a powerful family, and that although he may not be as powerful as his father he still has a lot of potential.

These eyes however were pure red, suggesting that this being is extremely powerful. It matters not which family she was born into it is merely her soul which is destined for greatness. She has been chosen for something and the gods have granted her power beyond belief to assist her with her task. The feminine vibe he felt from them however was unexplainable, how could he tell from just a pair of eyes floating in green stuff whether or not they were female?

And yet it was obvious by both the rush of unnecessary breath escaping his lungs and the beat of his heart as excitement hit him hard. Without seeing her or knowing anything about her Demetres interest was piqued. And he found himself desperate to know all that he could about this mysterious woman. He watched mesmerised as the eyes wandered closer, she drifted through the tree branches littering the shallow waters like an expert. As though it was some form of elegantly sexual art. His eyes were locked on the two red orbs floating through the water; over and under and round and through, disappearing then reappearing as though the hard and sturdy tree branches were nothing but ribbon that moulded around her as she swayed. He could see movement of limbs but no detail, the ripples in the water succeeding to hide everything about her except that she was there.

He watched as the eyes stopped moving, and a hand reached out of the water clinging to a rock jutting out of the cliff edge. He registered the long colourful fingers as they escaped the soft water to grasp the hard rock making all kinds of ideas come to mind. The skin on the hand reflected every colour imaginable and more, and although it should look grotesque and alien it looked elegant and amazing.

His eyes widened as the hand was followed slowly by the top of a head, green hair slicked back as she rose from the icy prison of the sea and inhaled deeply, her first breath of fresh air. Or so it looked to Demetre. To him it was as though everything was in slow motion, she may as well have a bathing suit on in the shower pursing her lips for a camera for what she was doing to him already! The site of her almost making him pant like a dog and he could barely contain himself as he rose up and leaned as far over as he could to take in the beauty of the creature he had heard of many times but never seen before.

Her entire torso emerged, and Demetre took in the entire site of her with more than appreciation or want. He found desire in him he never knew existed. He desired this woman, craved her even.

Her green hair; explaining why he couldn't see through the green leaves in the water, was slick back and reaching to about her waste. It was an extremely beautiful contrast to the red of her large and wondrous eyes. Blue lips as though she was freezing cold and yet they looked warm enough to kiss, her arms changing from the bluish silver colour at her shoulders to her elbow where the many colours started he witnessed before on her hand still holding the rock. Her legs drifting behind her are the same as her arms, long and colour full, with the toes long and webbed as though fins and feet moulded together. The patterns on her body commonly confused with scales was alluring, black lines all over her body swirling in patterns to encase her breasts and stopping at the top of her neck, then little patterns around her eyes. The entire scene before him looked like some kind of fantastically attractive monster. When his eyes fixed on her face he saw the prominent cheek bones, the way her hair started from further back than average, the way her human nose wasn't there. Instead were two slits at the side of where her nose should be, and still her beauty was so great he wanted to jump down and kiss her. She moved from one branch to another with so much finesse he wondered if she was just a figment of his imagination.

He longed to put his hands on her hips even though she was so tall from the waste up alone that this would probably bring him face to face with her breasts, which were so delectable he felt he may explode should he not get to touch them soon. He needed to explore this woman, to nibble her slightly pointed ears, kiss her long smooth neck, he needed to make love to this woman. He needed to hear her scream his name in ecstasy before holding her and keeping her safe. He wanted to protect her.

Her eyes roamed the clearing as though searching for something and for a moment Demetre wished they were searching for him.

She lifted an empty beer bottle the teenagers had left behind and examined it, looking at it from every angle and even trying to examine her hand through it as though seeing through a magnifying glass. She blew into it, listened to it and waited but she could not understand the attraction. In the end she threw it to the beach and focused on a cigarette butt hidden within some leaves on one of the rocks jutting out of the cliff. She must have been watching the humans because she lifted it to where her nose should be and grimaced, again throwing it to the beach as though to give the humans there vile rubbish back.

He saw all of her beauty exposed as her mouth fell open to examine something hanging from a tree branch. The moonlight reflecting from its mirrored surface as he fixated on the small vial like pendant hanging from the branches to her side, her hand raised to examine it and touch it and she smiled the tiniest smile at the feel of the chain on her fingers. Even though the smile was tiny, it was enough to make

Demetres heart flutter and he vowed to see that smile travel all the way to her eyes.

"I smell you up there Vampire. Know this, I am here to research the humans and that is all. Should you wish to cause me danger you will find yourself surprised." Her voice was magically amplified, bouncing off the cliffs edge and the trees surrounding. Demetre couldn't help but to raise his head and look around him in awe. Yet the softness of the voice rid him of any fear he might have been feeling. She is trying to be intimidating but she isn't really scared.

A wave crashed into the cliff edge near Demetre, not close enough for him to be in any danger but close enough for him to be sprayed with water. "Are you going to sit there watching me all night? Only if you are I would much prefer that you be of some use. What can you tell me of this?" She nods her head to the locket, the whole time she spoke she had not taken her eyes from it and yet her voice had him frozen with admiration as the power still radiated from the trees. After a few moments she turned to face him with one perfectly patterned eye brow arched in a question.

Demetre dropped from the sanctuary of his branch until he was almost level with her, even though she still had her legs in the water. He was transfixed by the patterns all over her body. His hand reached out as though to touch her and she looked from his hand to his face with a scowl, aggressively moving her hand back out of his reach.

"I don't mean to try to harm you!" Demetre says, holding his hands up. "I just … wanted to feel you."

"You think you have earnt that right? You think I do not feel as you do?" she spits at him, reminding him that this creature is not the same as him and may have different rules, for instance she may be very offended by his forward manner.

"Your right, I apologise. I found you so magnificent that the feel of your skin became the only thought on my mind. I am sorry to have offended you." He said sincerely, bending down and picking up the locket in his hand. He unclasped it and put it around his own neck to show her. "The humans wear them for decoration. Some have reasons such as it belonged to a loved one before they left for the other realm or it was bought by their lover for them. For others such as this cheap thing it was simply bought because it looked pretty and the owner wanted it."

"How do you know it was meaningless?" she asked.

"Because firstly she wore it out tonight, knowing she would take it off to get in the sea so it wouldn't snag on a branch and endanger her, the others remove there's for the same reason. And secondly because she left it here." He shrugged. He removed the necklace and held it out to her dangling from his fingers, she didn't take it. Instead she lifted her hand and continued to play with the chains hanging between his fingers.

For some reason the tiny sensation of the chain against his skin moving softly had him swallowing loudly, and she looked up at him as though in question. She backed away slowly with her head held downwards.

"I'm sorry, I forget how ugly I am to Walkers. I should leave." She whispers and starts to turn.

"No." he cries, his free hand reaching out to hold her arm and stop her leaving. As their skin touches a fire ignites, coursing through his veins and making him take a deep shaky breath. She recoils as though he has struck her, free hand going to rub the skin he just touched as though a bad burn while she gapes at him in wonder. "Please don't go." He begs and she moves back towards him curiously.

"Why?" she asks.

"I don't know, and I don't particularly want to." He answers.

"Well, that's an enigma."

"How so?"

"I am an ugly creature whom should never be allowed to walk the earth in fear my appearance would render some so frightened they would die from it, I am a creature of water you of night from both we are not welcome with the other, and we know nothing of each other not even our names for we have only just met. And you wish for me to stay? And you don't know why you wish it *and* you refuse to ponder the fact, afraid of what you will find." She states as though the whole thing sounds ridiculous, because it does.

"You are not ugly, you hold the entire beauty of a rainbow in the sky within your very flesh. Your patterns are mesmerising, they make me want to explore every inch of you to see what images are hidden within it like the shark on your shoulder and the starfish on your right breast. Your eyes have so much depth I feel I could lose myself within them and never have to come back to the real world again." by the time he finishes speaking he has the necklace around her neck and the clasp closed. Her eyes wide as she takes in every word he says, but he isn't looking at her eyes at that moment. He is staring at the small pendant now hanging perfectly between her breasts.

He is standing so close to her there is barely an inch between them and he looks up at her, arms holding hers with a desperate look on his face as his eyes scan hers for a reaction. She continues to just look lost until his mouth crashes down to hers.

In the back of his mind Demetre notes that while she is completely unresponsive and not kissing him back, she is also not pushing him away. Which must be a good sign. After just a few moments these thoughts are pushed from his mind and replaced with how soft her skin feels, how exciting it would be to put his arms around her waist and re-enact the event that happened in this little cove just a short while ago with the humans. He starts kissing her with more passion than nerves and she relaxes into it. Moaning slightly as her arms go up to wrap around his neck and her body collides with him as she matches him in need and want right there. Half in the sea and half out of it. She pulls him backwards so she falls back with him on top of her, crashing into the sea. Demetre doesn't mind, it adds to the spontaneity of this meet. He feels her fingers through his hair gently scratching away at his flesh as though to pull him even closer than he already is. Their bodies twisting and turning under the water as her tongue reaches out to touch his lips, asking permition to explore more of him. This time *he* moans and opens his mouth. Their bodies twisting together with hunger for one another as they glide through the calm of the current.

By the time they separate they are both dazed and confused, and after a moment or two when their eyes meet Demetre sees the panic etched upon her face.

Susan Hatton

Forbidden Love

Chapter 3.

"What does this mean?" she asks him seriously after they break the rippling surface of the water.

"Does it really matter?" he asks wading back towards her as she floats with only her head above the tiny waves. The reflective surface letting him see all her beauty doubled. The stars surrounding her making her look like a scene from a movie with how perfect she looks right there.

He takes her head in his hands and brings his face to hers again, kissing her cheeks and forehead and anywhere he can. "I never want to stop kissing you."

She closes her eyes and leans into his kisses, enjoying the warmth of another's flesh so close after years of being told love will never find her. Her mother would explode if she found out Alliyana was currently with a vampire. All those years of hatred as our mermaids went to war, all those lives lost to a battle that nobody started. Her mother trying to drill into her daughter that we have to hate the vampires but never giving her any other reason than "Because they are killing us.", as though they weren't also sending soldiers to battle.

She opened her eyes to take in the full view of him, the dark black hair and brown eyes, the tiny red ring around the pupils telling her he comes from a great and powerful family and has potential to be very powerful. The way his hair seems to tickle his ears and he shakes his head to throw it backwards. She lifts her hand and rests it lovingly on his cheek, caressing his skin with her thumb and taking in every imperfection from the mole on his neck to the slanting of one brow, barely noticeable from a distance yet up close she couldn't help but run her fingers along the smoothness of the tiny wet hairs.

"I thought I would never find love and here I am. I thought I was doomed to spend eternity with no one by my side." He closes his eyes again and lay his forehead on hers as though speaking the words out loud has rid him of a giant burden.

"As did I. but I still don't know what this means. I cannot love a vampire, it is not allowed." She had whispered more to herself.

It was a vampire that had caused the rift between her and her mother, a vampire that took her father from them. While she remained plutonic with the war she still hated that vampires had stolen her father from her and destroyed her happy childhood. How could she ever face anyone in the caves if they found out she was kissing one?

"I, Demetre Dracula, pledge everything I am and everything I have inside of me, to you." He was giving himself to her there and then, he knew no matter what happened he would always love her for this moment. For showing him love when he doubted he would ever feel it.

She had stilled when she heard his name, thinking how stupid she was for allowing him to fool her. She drifted out of his reach with eyes so angry they could burn the trees.

"Demetre *Dracula*?" she had repeated his name as though it were the very essence of the fire from which spurred her hatred. "You are a Dracula? Oh how could I be so blind, how could I let myself be tricked. How did I not plan for this?" Demetre looked at her with a mixture of confusion and hurt. How could she go from loving him to hating him just over a name? Surely she couldn't be that shallow, she was just kissing him knowing that he was a vampire!

"Wait, what is happening?" he asks confused as he tries to figure out what he has done wrong but keeps coming up with nothing. "My name does not define who I am inside, I will gladly drop it for you. No, I will throw it to the sharks with a smile on my face if it would make you happy." he tries to follow her, to catch her up and take her in his arms again only this time never let her go. But she flies backwards through the water starring daggers.

"I am Alliyana, daughter of Alliya and Androwda." Demetre freezes with fear.

"No." he denies. "You can't be."

"Your father murdered my father many years ago, and now you come for more blood on your family's vile hands." The air around them crackles as her hair starts to fly, Alliyana is rising out of the water showing Demetre her power is about to be unleashed as her eyes cloud over in darkness. Water cascading around him in magnificent waves pounding and crashing menacingly. The air above them becoming tense and bitter as lightning bolts racing across the sky.

"No please, Alliyana don't be angry with me. I am sorry for your father truly I am." he cries out to her over the sounds desperate for her to hear the begging in his voice, to know that he wishes things were different.

"You are afraid of me, vampire? Good. You should be." Her voice booms like the thunder around them and her patterns start to glow red.

"My only fear is that I have upset you. My father sickens me, he is not the same person as me please do not think that. I know it means little but I am sorry, I can't bear to think what you must have gone through at the hand of my selfish father. I hate that I carry his name."

"Leave me now, or feel my vengeance Vampire. There will be none of *my* blood spilled here tonight." Her threat very clear that if he doesn't leave she will not stop herself from killing him.

"I will not. If my death is what you need then I offer it freely, I love you Alliyana and I am sorry that causes you more pain. Take my life if you wish to have it, because to leave here and never see you again would be more pain than I can handle." She stares at him with her mouth open and eyes wide as he rips his shirt from his body and climbs onto the nearest tree branch. He kneels before the magnificent site of her surrounded by power. "I give myself to you Alliyana. My family took a life from you and I offer you mine in return. I know it won't fix this and it won't bring your father back. But it is all I have to give you." Tears spring from her eyes, mind working over and over to try and make sense of things. Here sits the son of the man who killed her father and destroyed her family, and she can't bring herself to harm a single hair on his head. How can she ever take over as ruler when her mother dies?

She lowers back into the water and Demetre is relieved to see the sky and waters calm, but when he looks at her and sees the hurt on her face he realises angry was better than sad. She cries silently while staring at him, tears streaming down her face and falling to mingle with the sloshing waves.

"I don't know what to say that will help, I don't want to make it any worse." He says.

"Stop talking!" She commands and he does, giving her a few moments to let this information sink in.

"I am princess of the sea, I am to be married in three weeks' time! It is the law that I wed before I take over as ruler of the seas. I have been battling my mother for years that I should choose my own husband. She will have me marry the first male she sees if she has to rather than change that stupid law. I have searched for love for many years and was almost about ready to give up, to accept that the closest I could get would be to watch the humans. You turn up randomly and show me what it might be like to love, making me believe we are both feeling the same things and then tell me you are the son of the man who murdered my father and that you want nothing to do with him at all. How can I ever trust you? How will I ever be able to believe a word from your mouth? Why should I not just turn and swim away now?" he lowers her head knowing the truth of her words and feeling them slice through him like a knife. The look in her eyes as though he had shown her the world and taken it away from her. Which he had.

He had shown her the love and passion that he felt for her, and shown her that she can be loved. And then he ruined it all by being a Dracula. It was his turn to shed tears, and although it looked to cause her pain, she didn't flinch from his hand reaching to wipe her tears.

"There are no reasons. I am sorry for all I have done and said tonight Alliyana. I guess we night creatures really are never meant to find love. This must be our punishment for trying to find what we weren't supposed to have." He sobs, knowing it isn't what a Dracula does but not caring. He feels like he could scream his pain to the moon. As he lets her go the water around them starts to ripple, swirling around them creating a whirl pool. Demetre looks at Alliyana.

"It's not me." She shrugs obviously as surprised as he is. A gust of wind blows the tree branches apart to give them a perfect view of the starry sky and they both gasp as a woman steps from the bark of a tree in front of them. Alliyana is the first to bow her head while Demetre just continues to stare with his mouth hanging open. She wears no clothes but instead of look sexual she looks natural. Her dark skin and dark hair looking blemished like any other humans and he knows that is true perfection. As with the humans and the tree trunks there must be differences.

"Mother." Alliyana whispers, not to her birth mother but to the mother of nature.

"Call me Mut please, it was my name in Egypt and it was my faverout."

"Forgive me."

"Not nessacary my darling." Mut smiles and raises Alliyana's head to look into her eyes. "You have caused no offense here." She reassures her.

Mut changes her attention to Demetre, who quickly bows his head in acknowledgement.

"Apologies Mut, I thought my kind unworthy of your magnificent presence." Again Mut raises his chin to look into her eyes.

"You can only think what you have been told my son, but I assure you it is quite the opposite. Should any vampire ask my help I would gladly give it, whether it was the help they asked for or not. Some of the ancients did not like that and instead preferred to ignore my existence."

"So you haven't given up on us?" he asks quietly in shock.

"Never." She replies. "Alliyana did you not wish for love?" she asks gesturing towards Demetre.

"Yes Mut, but how can I be sure that he is who he says he is and his feelings are true. How can I forget that his father murdered mine?"

"You mustn't." Is the answer. "Look into his eyes, do you believe he is lying about how he feels?" Alliyana turns to Demetre, the entire weight of the world staring back at her.

"No, I don't think he is lying." Her voice is full of hurt and pain. "But I can't forget about my father."

"Nobody wants you to my darling. Your father died in the war between mermaids and vampires, I think he would be more happy to move on should he see that war end." Her words are deep.

Demetre looks puzzled as Alliyana gasps and puts her hand to her mouth.

"What is it? Alliyana?" he asks worried.

"They want us to end the war." She barely whispers the words yet the carry through the clearing and seem to erupt another gust of wind, sending butterflies fluttering from the trees down to them. The water starts gushing and sloshing at their waists as the noise of the wind seems to whistle through the trees. Another whirlpool forms of fish instead of water some feet away from them. A woman rises from the water with long red hair and green eyes, Demetre smiles at the opposites as Alliyana has green hair and red eyes.

Her hair is platted to one side and falls to her breasts, which are covered with a white strip of material reaching all the way down to her knees and clasped at one shoulder with a gold broach.

"Serapheena, it is nice to see you again." Nods Mut as she welcomes this goddess into their circle.

"Thank you great mother." Serapheena bows before turning to Demetre and Alliyana.

"Do you know who I am?" she asks them and they both look ashamed to shake their heads. But Serapheena smiles warmly at them both and wraps them within her embrace, laughing light heartedly to let them know everything is ok.

"I am Serapheena, goddess of love. And you two are very important to me. I have been watching you both for years."

She removes her hand from Demetres shoulder and takes both of Alliyana's hands in hers. "You are destined to rule the sea my love, and you will be fantastic. Trust me you have nothing to worry about. You have been searching for a love you craved, a love you needed. But most important it is a love the sea needs." She turns her to watch the waters. "Your mother lost her husband and was thrust into the role of queen with no time to mourn. She lost herself, as did the others under her charge and the entire sea lost the beauty of their rulers. It has been dark and dreary to watch for the last few years as your mother tried to fix her broken heart, do not blame her for the way she been. It was not really her, remember that. Always remember that."

Now she turned to Demetre and took his hands. "And you love, you are the spawn of the man that started this war. It is expected that you marry Essy Valentine, who would be shunned by her family if she follows her heart, and take over your fathers place as commander in this war. Your parents I cannot explain. They simply do not feel love. It has been replaced with greed and envy and now is the time to turn things around. More will follow you than you think."

Serapheena put their hands together and placed her hands around them both.

"I bless this union with all that I am and all that will be, they must have the courage to fight their battles together as one, to love through the hate and to never lose sight of the end achievement." Demetre notices the tears on Serapheenas cheeks and for some reason lifts his hand to wipe them away.

"No." She says forcefully. "This is the only woman who should ever feel your loving caress, until you have a daughter." Alliyana sobbed at that moment, and Serapheenas eyes widened happily.

"Fertility is a gift I will give freely, in abundance to you and your daughters. And your daughter's daughter's and so on. For you two this task will be great, it will be tough and it will be emotionally devastating at times. And you will have boons from all of the greats for your sacrifices."

Alliyana turns to face Demetre, eyes full of excitement.

"Don't go choosing names just yet. We have the fight ahead of us first." He laughs and kisses her passionately. When they stop and turn back to Serapheena she is crying again, but she cries with joy and embraces them both again.

"You also have my blessing." Says Mut from behind them. "Alliyana I know you will need to remember that more than Demetre in the next few days." She embraces them as Serapheena did and then they both leave, giving Alliyana and Demetre time together.

Alliyana starts to cry, with both happiness and sadness in her eyes as her head finds Demetres shoulder. He strokes her hair and kisses her head telling her he will protect her.

Demetre nudges Alliyana awake, she mumbles and protests and he kisses the hand on his chest which is still bare from devoting himself to her.

"Alliyana you have to wake up darling." He whispers to her. "The sun is coming up. I wish we could stay here forever, but we both have things to do my love." He says quietly while still kissing her.

She turns and looks all around her before looking at Demetre. "I fell asleep?"

"You fell asleep." He repeats in answer to her question. "And now it's time to go. I can't hide in the sun light and we both have far much going on already than to be discovered by humans. We can meet here again tonight at sun set, I will keep all humans away." He leaves the water and grabs his shirt, then throws it after seeing how irreparable it is and for the first time Alliyana really looks at his body.

Demetre sees her staring and stands, attention fixated to the look of want she gives him. He walks back into the water towards her and without hesitation kisses her on the lips, taking her in his arms and protecting her as she accepts and returns his kiss vigorously. They are only pulled apart by the spot of sun light forming in the trees above, to which Demetre growls and pulls away angrily.

"Go before I can't take it any longer and follow you into the water!" he says and she smiles at how much self-control he has. She looks down to the bulge in his pants and her eyes widen as she gasps.

"Don't you even dare, I can't take any more teasing. Go or find someplace private for us to spend the day!" he warns. She turns and swims away, grinning to herself as an idea comes to her mind.

Susan Hatton

Chapter 4.

Alliyana swam home with a grin she couldn't lose. She knew the battle ahead would be hard and long, but she also knew that Demetre loved her and she loved him. And she would hopefully be doing her father proud and ending this wretched war. She swam past fish that turned and followed her, clearly excited to see the princess so happy as they rubbed themselves against her like pets in need of attention.

She stopped swimming for a moment and turned, closing her eyes and allowing the happy fish to swim all around her. Surrounded by the colours and strength of these sea creatures she feels her own strength increase, she feels happy and free and ready to fight. She can almost hear them professing the love for their princess and how nice it is to see her out of the caves. She lifts her hand and strokes a few of the fish causing them to shiver and wiggle faster, caressing them like a loving mother would a child before she begins to swim again.

Demetre wants privacy for them and Alliyana has decided that instead of starting her battle then and there she would wait and give herself a little time to come up with a plan of action. She knows her kind will abandon her unless she is queen. But she must be married to become queen, unless her mother dies which Alliyana can't even bring herself to think about. So her options are to not marry a mermaid and save herself for Demetre, in which case she will never be queen and yet Serapheena made it clear that she will be, or she must marry a mermaid and become queen before admitting her love for Demetre. In which case she will already be married when they are finally able to be together! The entire situation really needed some thinking, and she needed some time to explore the emotions running riot inside her over Demetre.

As she thought about him her smile grew wider. She would show him a little secret cave tonight and have the sea creatures help to keep them private. They would never judge her, they would never disown her for loving someone. The sea had always loved her and to some extent had taken over the affectionate motherly role when her father had died. She would fight a lot with her mother and swim off in anger. The sea would always send a friend to calm her. It was as though the sea was sorry for her, like it knew exactly what she was going through.

She became more and more excited as she began to plan their evening together, she would meet him at their cove and from there they would swim together to the hidden cave a few miles away. It was so perfect, they could have some time together to explore their feelings before the trouble started.

Alliyana was so busy thinking about what they could be getting up to in that cave that she didn't realise she had made it back to the caves of Miaya until she was almost out of them, she stopped in shock as she took in her surroundings. Everything *looked* to be in order yet something inside her told to be cautious. The cave was illuminated with creatures that glowed all different colours. The twists and turns enough to confuse any human should they ever find a way of exploring such deep waters yet to a mermaid are no problem at all. The hard rock walls softened by the plants that grow along them making it both welcoming and homely. Alliyana swam slowly out of the cave and into her home city under the water.

She swam through the opening leading her out of the maze of caves, and into the gigantic bowl of a city within the rocks. The ceiling covered with luminous plants and creatures, enough to light it up for everyone to see clear as day. There were no buildings or places to go just sea plants to use for seating or for catching food. The sea was a calm and easy living place. The mermaids ate fish as well as plants, but when they died there bodies would be left outside the caves to give back that which it took. It is only fair after all to give something back to others when you are done with it. The mermaids would gather in the open space for games and parties or just general chatter and fun, then they would return to the caves scattered within the walls enclosing the area.

Alliyana noticed the crowds of mermaids whispering and gossiping, quieting as soon as she came close enough to hear them. Thousands of mermaids turned to stare at her, all bowing their heads respectfully to her making Alliyana worry. The last time she had seen this many mermaids staring at her had been when her father had been killed.

"Mother." She cried worriedly and shot through the waters to find the cave in which she and her mother lived.

"Alliyana wait." Someone cried from behind her. But Alliyana kept swimming, desperate to find her mother and make sure she was ok. She passed by dozens of mermaids by the time she arrived at her home. They had no need for doors, they were furnished with other creatures of the sea. Various plants to make their beds or seats grew in abundance around the entire under water city making it a spectacular site filled with all different colours imaginable.

She entered the cave opening, calling her mother as she did.

"Oh Alliyana, I am so glad you're here. I have news for you!" her mother cried, rounding a corner to find her daughter panicking and crying. "Why whatever is the matter child!"

"Mother!" She cries relieved. "I was so scared, I saw everyone gathered and thought the worst. I'm so glad you're safe!" she threw her arms around her mother and cried with happiness, until her mother started pulling her off awkwardly.

"Yes well as you can see I am perfectly fine." Her mother answered matter of factly. "Now sort yourself out child, we have company!" she scolds. Alliyana looks at her mother hurt and confused, she thought her mother dead for a moment and was so relieved she wasn't that she had cried. She had at least expected her mother to smile and stroke her hair, to tell her everything was fine. But nothing. She straightened and looked her mother in the eye.

"I apologise mother. I guess you dying clearly is not as big a deal to you as it is to me."

"Don't be snide daughter this is neither the time nor the place. Now come and meet Jullian." She followed her mother with furrowed brows, not understanding why she would have to meet this man. She never met any of her mother's play things.

"Alliyana this is Jullian, Jullian this is my daughter Alliyana." She introduced them, Jullian took her left hand in his right, and put his left hand on her shoulder. A sign of respect in the small home of Miaya.

"A pleasure to meet you Alliyana. You are just as beautiful as your mother." He smiled at her.

"I'm sure. Mother, what is the meaning of this?"

"Well I thought you two should be introduced since you are going to be spending so much time together wedding planning." Her mother winked at her.

"Wedding planning?" she asked and turned to look at Jullian, this time noting the triumphant smile on his slightly wrinkled face, the depth within his eyes that seem to hold a darkness she was not willing to explore, the way his hair was slicked to the side instead of straight back like most peoples, probably to cover where it is starting to recede or thin out.

"You are to be my wife, and I your husband princess. I came here to offer myself to Miaya and your mother has graciously accepted. Our warriors will band together in the war such as our homes will band together in life." He beamed as though this statement should make her happy.

Alliyana snatched her hand from his and rid herself of the slimy feeling weight on her shoulder, leaving Jullian looking confused and her mother looking angry.

"You told me I could find my own husband." She spat at her mother.

"I told you that you may try daughter, but you are out of time. Your wedding is in two weeks. No more foolishness, you have responsibilities child and I will not let you run from them."

"How do I run from them mother? I am willing to accept being a ruler on my own. I am ready to conquer the heavens to protect those that live here, I am ready to sacrifice things in order to keep these people happy. What I am not prepared to sacrifice is my love. My heart. Without my heart I would not be the great ruler anyone here wants from me. I will not give it to the first stranger that offers his soldiers in battle!" She screams backing away.

"How dare you insult Jullian, he came here to offer himself as your husband so we might have a chance to win the war. Do you now want revenge for your father's death? I have no idea how I could have possibly brought up a daughter so selfish."

"This has clearly been a shock for the princess, I don't take any insult from today I shall just leave and give her some time to accept this. Alliyana I look forward to seeing you my dear, for now I shall start the plans for the wedding and let you have some time to deal with your emotions." His words are said kindly and her mother is obviously fooled by them.

She stares at Jullian with bright eyes and a smile that says 'That is so thoughtful!'

"I wouldn't bother. I am afraid your journey has been wasted, I am already engaged to another." She turns and swims away, leaving her mother alone with Jullian as she makes her way to her own private room. The one she knows not even her mother will enter as it holds to many memories of her father telling her stories at bed time. Alliyana loved to remember her father, but her mother hated it and wouldn't even speak his name. As though she was ashamed of the man she said she loved.

Alliyana threw herself onto the pile of seaweed she used for a bed and began to cry, memories of her father and the disappointment in her mother only adding to the emotional stress she had to deal with. All thoughts of her and Demetre having alone time gone for the next short while. Instead she cried to herself, and begged the goddess's that should they grant her a boon it be that her mother find happiness again and stop punishing her daughter for her own misery.

Susan Hatton

Chapter 5.

Demetre had walked home a complete happy wreck, he had gotten quite a few strange looks from people as he walked with soaking wet trousers and shoes and no top and a smile from ear to ear. He hadn't even been worried about the humans seeing him, instead he waved as he walked past the man delivering milk. He yelled "Good morning" at people on their way to or from work. He walked like he belonged as for the first time in his life that was exactly how he felt.

He walked in the front door of his home, and skipped up the stairs two at a time. All the while thinking how nice it felt to sink his mouth to Alliyana's, how good it would feel to do it again when he met her again that night.

"Demetre?" his mother called, appearing from one of the rooms as he arrived at the top of stairs. "Oh heavens what on earth have you been doing now? Good lord and it's already eight in the morning!" she looked panicky for a moment then cross. "Shower. Now! They will be here at nine!" she commanded and walked quickly away 'tutting' as she noticed the mess he had left on his way up the stairs. He leant over the balcony with a grin and yelled.

"It is only water and mud mother. Worse things have happened you know!" he turned and raced up the rest of the stairs, excited like a child at Christmas. Walking into his room he eyes the clothes laid out on the bed, running his finger up and down the material of the blue denim jeans and black short sleeved shirt, with silver poppers instead of buttons.

"Seriously mother you must think I am five years old choosing my clothes for me. He scooped the clothes up and threw them into the wardrobe opposite his large bed and flung himself to lay on top of the covers, looking all round him at the plain white walls and black curtains, black furniture and red bedding. Clearly his mother's tastes instead of his own, the only thing they had agreed on was the head board. The metal swirls captured his attention from day one, he had loved how the way the black swirls had curved up and around had looked like waves in the sea.

Demetre closed his eyes allowing his thoughts to wander again to the soft delicious skin of his lover, the way the waves licked at her skin and the way her eyes had wanted him before she left. How he had wanted her so much in that moment. He closed his eyes and felt himself grow within his wet trousers, which he just realised at that moment must be soaking his bed! He shot up awkwardly laughing at himself for being so distracted, and grabbing a towel he walked into his own private bathroom where he relieved himself of the frustration she had welled up inside of him in the only way he knew how.

After his shower he had dressed in a white shirt and black trousers, very formal for a very formal occasion. He checked himself out in the mirror and debated whether or not to change his shirt for a black waist coat with nothing underneath, his mother would just die if he chose to make such a statement against her while they had company. He smiled at the thought but stopped himself. That would just be childish. He ran his hand through his hair and left the safety of his bedroom.

He walked down the stairs to the dining room with his hand on the dark wood balcony, sweeping his hand over it and remembering the times he had climbed up and slid down. His mother had always gotten angry at his behaviour but not the way most mothers would.

"Demetre! Do you think this is how a Dracula should behave?" she had always asked him viciously, letting him know she didn't care if he had hurt himself, what if someone had seen him! His lips tilted to one side as half way down the ridiculously large staircase he flung one leg over the wood and slid all the way to the bottom where he fell off onto his back side laughing. When he looked up he was met with the evil eyes of his mother, the shocked and disgusted eyes of another woman and then just the shocked eyes of a much younger and attractive woman. Demetre smiled and laughed harder as he stood.

"Oh mother, one day your face will freeze like that you know. Then the entire world will see the dragon within!" his mother's mouth pulled together like she had eaten a sour lemon, the woman next to her gasped and pulled out a handkerchief to hold over her mouth as though ashamed and the woman behind them both laughed out loud, quickly disguising it as a cough.

"It is time for tea." Said his mother through her teeth and she stormed off, followed by the other easily offended woman as the third stood for a moment staring at him looking as though she had a lot on her mind.

"Well." She had said, clearly unsure of how much to tell him. "You must be Demetre." She had said almost reluctantly as though she really hoped he wasn't.

"Yes I am." he answered her.

"I am Essy Valentine. I have to say that was quite a show." She nods to the banister.

"My mother used to hate it when I was a child. I figure if she insists on treating me as one then I may as well play the part." He leans closer looking around to check she wasn't nearby he said quieter "And it's a lot of fun!"

"You seem interesting at least. I suppose tonight can't go as horrid as I thought." She smiled at him and he held out his arm to her smiling warmly.

"Come, I shall show you to the room where we stuff face. We like to ram food into our gaping holes in this house, although mother has perfected the art of making a dead animal disappear while chewing on its carcass look almost refined." She was chuckling away at his pretence to sound posh and snobbish, and when they entered the dining room it must have looked like they had immediately hit it off as the other two woman smiled knowingly at each other. Demetre and Essy's brows knit together in confusion at the pair as Demetre pulled out the chair next to Essy's mother for her to sit on, then went and sat beside his own mother.

"OK mother I do believe I am ready for the bad news now. What is the meaning of this? Normally when you lay out clothes for me and give me such a disgusted look of outrage it is because you had expectations. I really hoped you would have learnt by now."

"Demetre do close your mouth, you have no idea how childish you look tonight." She had snapped making him laugh out loud.

"I know exactly how childish I look mother." He replied while balancing a spoon on his nose. "Now tell me, why is this dinner important?" as he asked the question the doors opened and the servants began to bring plates and lay them on the table.

When a small woman with blonde hair placed a plate before Demetre he automatically said "Thank you Lillith." And smiled at her, making Lillith appear uncomfortable and the others around him gape yet again shocked by his action.

"Sir." Lillith bows her head respectfully and scutter's away.

"Demetre!" his mother scolds.

"Oh for fuck sake mother eat your dam food." He blanked the rest of the speech that spewed from his mother's mouth as he set into eating his food. All he heard was the occasional "I am so sorry for my sons behaviour tonight, he is not normally so disrespectful." When he had finished his food he finally looked up to see his mother had barely touched her food, same as Essy's mother and yet Essy was tucking in with great delight, clearly enjoying the meal in comfort. When the servants returned Demetre thanked them as did Essy, who beamed at him over the table. Her mother quickly gasped and looked about to cry.

"Essy, do not dare speak to the *servants* ever again. You know the trouble it causes." Her mother says quietly. Demetre stares daggers at Essy's mother over the way she had said the word servants as though it was a disease.

"Actually I am quite friendly with the servants here. Lillith is about my age, when mother forced me to learn to play the piano the only way I enjoyed it was to teach Lillith at the same time. We grew up like sisters, she was born from one of the servants and lived here with us. Very often I would sneak away to find her and play with as a child, and when the twins came along she accepted those as her friends too. Then she grew up and was told she was not allowed to speak with me anymore. People were too scared we might fall in love or something. Even friendship isn't allowed amongst our kind is it mother?"

"Enough!" yelled his mother.

"I agree." He stood and made to leave, his mother's words stopped him as the evil dripped from her voice.

"Essy is to be your wife Demetre. Between the four of us she has shamed her family as much as you shame this one. Now you both will do as you are told you little brats because I swear if you walk out that door now Demetre you will never be allowed back through it again!"

Demetre takes a deep steadying breath before turning around, he sees Essy looking at her own knee and crying to herself. He walks over to her and takes her hand, pulling her to standing so he can look in her eyes.

"Essy I cannot marry you. I do not want to marry you. You deserve someone to love you and take care of you for the rest of your life." He lifts his chin with his fingers the same caring way Serapheena had to him and Alliyana. "I already have found my love." He answers and kisses her forehead like a friend would.

"You see child, now nobody will have you!" says Essy's mother in a panic. "Nobody wants damaged goods but do you care? No!" she stands and throws her handkerchief in her hand bag and gets ready to pull her daughter behind her.

"Excuse me? What the hell has happened to us vampires? She is your daughter!" Demetre yells taking Essy and standing before her.

"She is a burden on my existence, if you knew the trouble she has caused you wouldn't wish to defend her."

"What could possibly be so bad?" he asked threateningly.

"She had sex with her maid!" spat her mother disgusted. Demetre freezes and turns to her questioningly.

"I am in love with a female." He instantly hates the way Essy drops her eyes to the floor ashamed of herself.

"That is it?" he asks making every woman in the room snap their heads around to stare at him.

"It does not disgust you?" asked Essy.

"Trust me, I am in no place to comment on forbidden love!" he laughs and turns to his mother.

"Mother I am in love, I have found a woman I feel strongly for and I shall marry her. Whether that is in two weeks or two years I don't care. I do not wish to stay here, I would rather hide in the shadows of day than stay any longer in this wretched house with you." As he speaks the door opens to the kitchen, and out walks a number of servants who had clearly been standing listening. They all remove their aprons and hand them to Driana as they move to stand with Demetre.

"It's about time!" says Lilith smiling at him.

"Where do you think you are all going?"

"With Demetre, we only stayed for him and the twins. And the twins aren't here anymore anyway! You sent those off as soon as the nappies started smelling." Lillith turned to Demetre. "We are ready to follow you, we will help you with anything you need." She knew, they all knew that when Demetre took over the war would end. Demetre almost starts to cry, but instead he hugs Lillith and pulls Essy out of the door as the others follow.

"Who is she?" Asks Essy when they reach the privacy of the street and the servants all turn wide eyed at Demetre also wanting to know.

He takes a deep breath. "Alliyana, princess of the sea." Everyone around him freezes except Lillith who gushes.

"Oh it's like a story book!" And Demetre laughs. He notices the smile on their faces as they all instantly accept his forbidden love.

"I was wrong. We vampires aren't doomed after all."

Chapter 6.

Alliyana woke from a restful sleep filled with dreams of Demetres arms around her, they kept her usual waking's away and she found once she had fallen asleep she had not woken until well after everyone else had. She left her bed with a smile on her face and only a vague recollection of her encounter with her mother and Jullian. It didn't matter, she was going to marry Demetre instead. Somehow. She swam excitedly from her bed chamber, already eager to get through the day and enjoy her night.

Her mother was already done with breakfast by the time Alliyana appeared in the dining hall. The stone room much like the others in their cave was vast, and it had a cold and empty feeling to it now nobody was there but her. She knew her mother would find her at some point in the day to discuss the marriage. But she didn't care.

She took a seat and tasted some of the foods before her, her mind elsewhere as she contemplated the prawns and the oysters on the end of the stone slab table carved by soldiers on the ancient Bermuda triangle. The place where humans magically get lost so not to find the many mermaids who visited the island. To walk on land, find materials, some even go there to holiday!

The food was always the same in Miaya, it grew very boring very quickly. Alliyana had swam past the islands before and seen mermaids with fruits of all colours and shapes, biting into them as a look of extreme pleasure crossed their faces. She longed to try land food. The colours looked delicious!

But her mother never allowed her on any land, her father had died on land. Last night was the closest to walking on the land she had ever got, hiding amongst the trees and branches to watch humans frolic and play without a care in the world.

She remembered the humans that made love before her, and how entrancing it was to watch them. She closed her eyes remembering how much the woman seemed to enjoy what they were doing, and how good she had felt when Demetre had kissed her. She had been lost within a whirlwind of her own lust and allowed him to devour her mouth. Her tongue crept out to lick her lips at the memory, hoping to find a small taste of him still lingering. Her hand went to rub her neck and she felt the small chain from the necklace he had placed around her neck. In the back of her mind she noted how it had become like a piece of her already, the small vial dangling between her breasts hadn't gotten in her way once since.

She imagined it was his tongue tasting her lips instead of her own, and his hand rubbing her neck. She imagined it was him doing those things to her body that the humans were doing, with those eyes so full of need and want for her. She felt herself heat up at the thought as her other hand rested itself on her stomach, ready to explore where she wanted him to explore.

"I had hoped to find you alone." The voice made her jump. She stood quickly; embarrassed to be caught so distracted, to see who it was spying on her. Jullian was hovering in the entrance to the hall with a strange look on his face that made Alliyana feel very afraid. "I did not mean to startle you princess. I meant only to apologise again for last night. The meeting did not exactly go as I had planned either."

"And how did you plan for it to go exactly? 'Alliyana come meet this man, there you have laid eyes upon each other and not recoiled in horror. The wedding is set for two weeks.' And I would be overjoyed? The thought of marrying for duty is not the future I had planned for myself."

"But you knew all your life that you would have to marry before your nineteenth birthday. Please understand princess, I have a family honour to keep as well. I am simply curious as to how one can throw away everything her parents had worked so hard for on some silly belief of finding love." His words are harsh but the look of hunger in his eyes showed her exactly what was on his mind.

"My father did not fight so that I would be forced into marriage, he did not die for the great honour of having his daughter never know love. Let me put it another way. We are not getting married. And you need to leave." He enters the room and comes closer to her but she backs away slowly, covering her breasts with her arms and feeling very uncomfortable. Jullian's arms shoot towards her grabbing her wrists painfully and she cries out a little in shock.

"Princess, I must warn you that you tread dangerous waters here. There is more at stake than you believe. I want this marriage to go smoothly for the both of us but I am prepared to do whatever is necessary to get where I want to be. And I suggest you stop looking quite so lost in yourself as you touch yourself in future, or I might not be able to refrain myself from taking what I want." He leans close, so close she can almost taste his breath and she shivers with fear and disgust. "As for this other man, does he even exist?"

"GUARDS!" She screams, and he lets go as six very largely built men swim into the area within a matter of seconds. "Jullian is leaving, please escort him out and make sure he leaves the queens waters safely. And don't you forget Jullian, if you ever so much as harm me again there is more than the queen and these guards you will answer to." The guards take in her bruised wrists, and the words muttered to Jullian and remove him with extra force. She knows these men feel strongly to protect her, they respected her father very much and when he died they swore to take on the role of protecting her from harm. And that is exactly what they had done. She had watched as her mother became bitter and harsh towards them, and had started to show her own appreciation in the only way she could at such a young age. It had brought tears to their eyes as they all accepted her gifts to them, and they still wore their tiny sea shell necklaces she made with her own hands with pride with pride now.

"Come with us Jullian, we shall give you the guided tour." Spoke the largest of all the guards as they left with him trailing behind. He turned back around giving Alliyana a very nasty look, but she just smiled and waved her fingers at him before swimming off in the opposite direction as the guard behind thumped him in the back . "My apologies." He had said as though it was an accident and the others had laughed.

Alliyana swam through the caves curious as to what she could do to waste the day away until she could see Demetre. She swam and smiled, and span around in the water as though she danced. Her hand reached out to feel the sides of the tunnels and caves and she stopped regularly to appreciate the colours of the luminous animals and plants. After a short while she was sure it glowed brighter and cheerier!

"Alliyana is that you?" she heard her mother's voice and stopped smiling, she turned to meet the eyes staring at her disbelievingly.

"Good morning mother." She sighed.

"I think we had better have a talk, don't you?" she followed her mother into her private room, immediately disgusted by the amount of plants there are for seating in this room. Why on earth would one woman need all this?

"I still think this room is by far too full for you alone mother." She said looking around her. Her mother took a seat and leant all the way back, her arms spreading out to rest so she took up her more space than needed as Alliyana simply sat on her bottom.

"Don't be ridiculous Alliyana I am queen, I deserve the best don't I?" Alliyana didn't answer her. "Besides that is not why I asked you in here. Your behaviour yesterday was unforgivable, and I expect you to make a formal apology to Jullian."

"OK mother, I shall apologise to Jullian for him getting his hopes up and then being rejected. Should I also apologise for having him forcefully removed from our dining hall this morning as he perversely watched me, then grabbed me so I couldn't leave?" she held up her wrists.

"Oh goddess what have you done now!" was her mother's reply.

Alliyana raised from her seated position and swam from the room yelling "I have found love mother, you could be happier about it!"

Alliyana swam away from her mother and out of Miaya in record time, she swam far far away and decided to hide away and pass the day with the sea.

Chapter 7.

Demetre, Essy, Lillith and the other servants Demetre classed as his friends were stood outside his parent's house, wondering what their next move should be.

"I say we find your love." Demetre says to Essy and she lights up.

"Yes, lets!" she replies. "She lives a few short miles from here, mother and father had her banished when they found out about us. I was never ashamed of her, I just wanted to say that. I love Louissa so much. I feared what my parents would do to her if I tried to stand against them." she turned now Demetre. "Now I know that is cowardice, and the only way to change the way things are is to stand up and fight! There ARE vampires willing to accept same sex relationships!" she beamed and Demetre put his arm around her.

"Do you know something, I knew as soon as I laid eyes on you that we would get along. You're like a sister already!" they started walking down the street with the group of servants following behind them.

"Wait, Demetre wait here a moment." Lillith shouts and runs around the back of the house. When she returns she hands out coats and umbrellas as well as bottles of water. "It is the middle of summer, even a few short miles in this sun would be enough to put a vampire out for days."

"How thoughtful Lillith!" she hands a coat and bottle to Essy who pulls her in for a hug to say thanks, Lillith is the first to pull away looking uncomfortable but still happy.

"You like females too?" Demetre asks and she snaps around with her mouth wide open.

"She does!" Says Essy after seeing her reaction.

"Well…… I ……" Lillith closes her mouth and walks away from them, and Essy and Demetre start giggling a little bit.

"I guess there are more forbidden loves out there than I thought." Says Demetre thoughtfully as he starts walking to catch up with the others, Essy following behind. "She was right."

"Who was right?" she asks mildly interested.

"Huh? Oh, Serapheena appeared to me and Alliyana, she said that more people would follow my lead than I thought. I guess she was right." He continued to look thoughtful as Essy's brows raised in question.

"Serapheena?" she asks not knowing who this goddess is.

"Jeez, she has been forgotten about for far too long! Serapheena is the goddess of love." He informs her and Essy stops in her tracks.

"A goddess? A goddess appeared to you?" She says with a hint of sarcasm. "Everyone knows the greats don't bother with our kind!" she starts to sound almost angry.

"I promise you, both Serapheena and Mut showed themselves to us and gave us their blessing."

"I don't believe it." She says.

As they stand arguing about the goddess a gust of wind blows all around the vampires, it blows the leaves in swirling patterns around them and the trees start to knit together above them. A woman with long red hair and bright green eyes steps out from behind the trees.

Essy gasps as her eyes take in the beauty of this woman, but she quickly ducks her head back down ashamed.

"Do you think me attractive Essy Valentine?" Asks Serapheena, taking a step forward and revealing one leg through the sheer white material cascading down her body like a waterfall. The smooth and perfect skin decorated with a silver chain around her ankle and a single toe ring as she steps forward again towards the now shaking Essy.

"I find you beautiful goddess." Says Essy.

"But are you attracted to me?" she asks now so close their breasts are almost touching and Demetre can't help but watch with fascination as Serapheena reaches up and takes a strand of Essy's hair.

Essy's breathing has increased, as her eyes darted from the luscious red lips in front of her to the ample and inviting breasts just below. The skin smooth and light coloured, hair styled to perfection and eyes that burned to the very soul.

Serapheena stopped playing with the strand of hair, and instead laid her palm on Essy's chest to feel her heart beneath, but Essy was only thinking about how close it was to her breast.

"Do you wish to kiss me, Essy?" asked the goddess of love. And expelling a large breath of air she nodded her answer, to which the great goddess took her face within her soft hands and kissed Essy's lips. The tip of her tongue licking her lips slightly as Essy moaned and accepted her, opening her mouth and letting Serapheena take whatever she wanted.

Serapheena pulled away far quicker than Essy would have liked, this was evident in the anguished cry that escaped from the woman left panting for breath.

"Do you accept my gift of free will child?" Essy nodded vigorously. "Good, then don't ever be ashamed of your sexuality. Be pleased you actually have one!" The goddess gave her a wink and turned to leave, noting Demetre as he stood in the same place with his jaw almost on the floor watching the two women. She blew him a kiss and walked back into the trees.

"Wait Serapheena we have another one!" Yelled Demetre desperate for some more action. Alliyana had had much more of an effect on him than he realised! But the goddess kept swaying her hips as she walked away, clearly amused with how open Demetre is about his sexuality.

"Essy that was hot!" Says Demetre. When he turns he sees she is stood staring after the goddess with wonder in her eyes.

"She accepts me, and she loves me." She whispers, when she turns to Demetre she is crying happy tears. "All these years being told by my mother that nobody will ever love me or want me now that I am "damaged" the goddess herself accepts me and loves me. Gay or not!" She walks briskly away clearly eager to meet up with her love after her meeting with the goddess.

After walking for about twenty minutes Essy runs off and stops in front of a door of a rundown building. Demetre and the rest stop some distance away, giving Essy and her love some space to reunite.

Essy knocks on the door, and then knocks again before a woman in a silk dressing gown answers.

"Who's there?" she asks and freezes when she sees Essy.

"What are you doing here? Do you know the trouble you could get into?" Demetre is happy to know the woman cares more for Essy's safety than her own.

"I love you." Is her only response and she jumps into Louissa's arms and kisses her. Demetre watches as they embrace each other on the doorstep. That kiss so intense they forget about the public that could see and focus only on each other. When they pull apart the woman in the dressing gown notices Demetre and quickly moves to stand before Essy. She must have taken in his fancy clothes and perfect appearance and known straight away he was a vampire. And the crowd of around 12 others behind him couldn't have helped.

"Be gone from here, she has done nought wrong. I will take her back to her family and explain ... she must be ill. She may have a temperature."

"Lissy it's ok. He brought me here. And I have news. The goddess has blessed us. She accepts us."

Louissa looks from Essy to Demetre and back again.

"I think you need come inside." She murmurs to the both of them, still not trusting Demetre fully but he doesn't blame her. He enters her home and begins the explanation of what is happening and the great mother, and the battle they face to be accepted.

Chapter 8.

Alliyana is swimming around the islands, trying to catch a glimpse of the land. Images of grassy mountains and fluffy white clouds taking over her brain as she becomes desperate for distraction from waiting all day to see Demetre again.

"Alliyana!" she hears from behind her. She quickly turns around, instantly on alert as she is pulled from her thoughts.

"Hello Medea, is everything alright?" Alliyana asks her friend as she swims up to her side. Medea has been Alliyana's friend since they were children, and one of the few who Alliyana could rely on with her secrets growing up. Her long grey hair was floating behind her as Medea sped up to meet her friend. Medea's patterns much like the other mermaids were limited to her fore arms and her legs. Where Alliyana's patterns extended to her toes and fingers and danced around her breasts to look seductive and yet secretive. Nobody knew why Alliyana's patterns were so prominent, but with the colour of her eyes everybody just assumed it was another sign of power.

"Well I hope so. I hear you turned down Jullian for marriage. He is not someone you want as your enemy you know." The thought of marrying someone just because she would rather not be enemies with them had Alliyana shocked and appalled.

"Oh don't start. You know how I feel about marriage." She grew increasingly upset over the inability to allow someone to marry for love. Why did she need a husband to become ruler anyway? What was so important about have a male in her life to control her and threaten her?

"Yes, and so does everyone else." Medea said with her eyes burning into Alliyana.

"What's that supposed to mean? What exactly are you trying to say?" Alliyana grew impatient with all of the secrets. It was too much for her to keep up with.

"Just remember that we depend on you as the new ruler when your mother dies. And not everyone is so sure you are taking your role seriously. There is talk!" she whispers.

"So they think I'm committing treason because I want to fall in love? I have to suffer because of who my parents are? I am not allowed to marry in my time it must be forced on me whether I want it or not, whether I am ready or not? How about I become queen and enforce a law that says *every* female be married before she turns nineteen? That would mean you next, tell me Medea how do you like the idea of your parents choosing who *you* spend the rest of your life with." Alliyana spits harshly, angry that nobody believes she is entitled to true love just because she is a princess.

"I am just telling you what the others are saying, there is no need to be so childish!" Replies Medea becoming angry with her friends reaction.

"And what do you think of my life?" Alliyana challenges her friend, almost daring her to tell the truth.

Medea holds her head down as though ashamed. "I think you are thinking with your heart, and that is not the action of a princess. I think we need a ruler that is logical, that can put infatuation to the side and do as must be done. I think there is another war coming, and it is going to change all of our lives forever and for that we must be prepared." Medea raises her head and looks straight into Alliyana's eyes. "You must marry and take the throne, but you must follow your head and forget your heart Alliyana, or they will turn against you and seek the enemy as their friend. I hear some already are!" she whispers and quickly looks around her to make sure nobody heard her.

At first Alliyana becomes ashamed of herself for becoming so angry with her friend, by coming and speaking to her in the first place Medea is risking being shunned by everyone else. Alliyana has no right to be upset with her friend for worrying, it is a good thing that she puts the safety of everyone before her own selfish desires and tells Alliyana the truth risking being thawed out by her friends. It shows her loyalty to Alliyana that she can speak so openly. Then her words sink in and Alliyana's head snaps up to meet Medea's

"And by the enemy you mean?" asks Alliyana with eyes bright, sure that if there are mermaids already in league with the vampires then there job to change the minds of everyone around them must start there.

"I overheard Selia and his friends talking this morning about where to meet the land walkers. Some cove to the north, by nightfall they said. Tell the guards to follow them and arrest them for treason, that will earn you the trust of everyone again."

"Thank you Medea, you have no idea what you have just done. I am sorry friend for becoming so angry, and I thank you from the bottom of my heart that you can be so open with me when others feel the need to talk behind my back. Do you accept my apology?" Medea hugs her and nods. "Good, and know this. I am thinking with my heart, and I have it on word from the goddess that it is the right thing to do. You have to trust me." She hugs her friend again and swims quickly away, making her way to someplace private to call for Mut.

"Mut?" she asks lovingly to the corals around her and instantly she hears a voice from somewhere in the distance.

"Child speak, for I cannot be there in person at this moment and you are in no danger. What is troubling you?" asks the voice.

"Thank you for answering me Mut when so clearly are you busy, I hear some of the mermaids are already in league with the land walkers!" she pauses for a moment and although it is silent she is sure the water sighs with relief.

"So things have been set into motion for you." Whispers the voice excitedly.

"Please if possible, could you send word to Demetre somehow that he might meet me earlier than normal tonight? I believe we should be there to meet with them and earn their friendship."

"That is a very good idea my child. You are wise as your mother was, when she too was young and in love. Unfortunate actions can be the end of..." the voice cuts out and Alliyana begins to worry. "My child I must go, the sea has ears and I'm afraid we have been heard. Demetre is undertaking his own tasks and will not be able to come earlier tonight." The voice is low, for Alliyana's ears alone and she worries over who it is that has heard them, but when she goes to investigate she finds no one.

She wonders vaguely what could possibly keep Demetre from meeting her but quickly shrugs away her concern, he has the same battle as her to fight with his own family. Alliyana starts to swim back to Miaya in the hope of finding Selia and starting the task of winning over the revolution. Her thoughts running around her head of what to say.

When she arrives back through the caves she sees everything is normal, mermaids gather in groups to gossip and have fun in the large open area in the middle of all the homes built into the rock walls. She sees a group to the far left with Selia in the centre and rushes over to him.

"Selia, may I have a word?" she asks politely and although his brow creases he agrees, slipping away and into Alliyana's cave behind her.

"Is there something I can help you with princess?" he asks genuinely confused.

"I have heard things, about you meeting walkers." She whispers quietly to him and he recoils.

"I ... I don't know what you're talking about princess, I assure you I am being framed!" he replies in fear almost and she quickly raises her hands to show she isn't going to harm him.

"Please Selia, it is OK. I am too in league with a walker. A vampire." She whispers and Selia's eyes seem to scope her, trying to decide if she is telling the truth. She swims back to the entrance of the cave to make sure nobody is listening then returns to Selia. "It's true, I met him by the shore and we fell in love. I want the war to end too and not by winning it!" she says and this time he looks down at his hands in the water.

"Princess this is dangerous, I do not like to get you involved. I think we should both forget what we have heard today." Selia speaks as though almost regretful but clearly has a new found respect for his princess and he wants to keep her out of the danger he and the others are causing.

"Not an option." She replies and he stares at her. "I will be there tonight with Demetre, the vampire I love." He smiles at her and she puts her hand on his shoulder as a sign of respect. "I am more than a princess Selia. I am a heart."

"Thank you Alliyana." He lays his hand on top of hers and quickly bows his head before swimming from the cave, leaving her smiling and excited that already they have help on both sides!

Chapter 9.

Demetre can't stop looking out of the window waiting for the light to diminish enough so they can make their way to meet Alliyana. Essy and Louissa have been talking all day and Louissa is sceptical of what they are doing, worried it will endanger Essy. Essy obviously is not letting her talk her out of it.

"Essy this is dangerous, you should go back to your family and apologise, they will keep you safe." She would scold.

"No way, Demetre and the others will keep me safe. And if I die then I die for love. I risk my life in the hope of ending this ridiculous outrage on love. Love is worth fighting for." They kissed a lot and the others had thanked Louissa for the use of her home to shade them from the sun.

As soon as it became darker outside Demetre told them all to prefer themselves, and they left the safety of the home covered with coats and umbrellas so they wouldn't over heat, and water bottles full of ice water.

"Can you believe the humans think it is the rays of the sun that make us wither and die?" Asks Essy as they begin to walk towards the beach. The others laugh at the naivety of humans, the truth being that vampires need to stay extremely cool or they will dehydrate very easy. The sun makes the process speed up and while it won't kill them unless they are out for hours in sunlight with no shade or water it will slow them down and make them easier to kill. But then, if you leave a human in the desert with no shade or water they too will die.

They all keep walking, mumbling the odd conversation but the one who walks the fastest and seems the most eager is not Demetre, it is Lillith.

"I have always wondered about mermaids!" she called back when the others asked her to slow down for them.

When they arrive at the beach Demetre is the first to wade into the water and check the clearing, he sees Alliyana leaning against a tree looking lost in thought. She looks happy and eager, staring at the moon as it rises above the surface of the water. He enters the small clearing and she turns, smiling at him. She dives over to him as her mouth hungrily finds his and her hands stroke the back of his shoulders. He returns her kiss with a deep growl that has her smiling and giggling with her mouth still against his. He pulls away and devours her with his eyes.

"Soon darling. Trust me, soon." His eye brows raise as he drinks in her look of want and licks his lips before shaking his head. "First, I have a surprise for you. Come with me." He pulls her from the clearing and round to face the beach where she stops smiling and faces the vampires waiting for her.

"Demetre?" she asks unsure of what is happening.

"It is OK. They are on our side." He answers as he starts to bring her to shore. As she gets closer to the land she becomes very nervous.

"Demetre I cannot!" she tries to pull away but he smiles and kisses her again.

"You can." He assures her and she lets him pull her to the shallow water, her legs still flowing behind her as she lowers her arm, touching the sand underneath her. He lets her go as he stands and walks to the others completely drenched, and slowly she puts her legs down and thrusts her body out. In the water where Demetre could stand with just his head and shoulders out of the water she has her entire torso free, and she strides forward as she would on the sea floor.

"Wow." She hears the voice of a shy young vampire and looks to find the face grinning up at her. "I'm Lillith." She bows her head and the others start to bow as though reminded of who she is.

"No please, stop. You fight for us, you should never bow for me!" she says acknowledging that these vampires are offering themselves to help these two be together. Instead Alliyana bows her head to the group and the others giggle excitedly at the praise shown to them by a princess.

"Oh please Princess we are merely maids!" says one of them as her face turns slightly pink.

"Maids willing to give your lives for the good of others. That deserves respect!"

"It certainly does." Agrees Demetre. "And as a reward, when this battle is over I will do my best to make sure you never have to serve others again! Especially the likes of my mother."

"Darling the only reason we stayed so long was to care for you young uns. The twins are at boarding school now and only come home twice a year for a week! Let's hope and pray that they find their own way."

"They already have." Demetre smiles remembering the girl's antics.

Demetre turns to look up at Alliyana, who looks down at him barely the same height as her breasts.

"This may cause some problems. Biologically." He frowns and she laughs.

"We will figure it out!" she scolds and sits on the beach with her legs to one side, he sits next to her and gazes out at the site before him. The moon on the ocean.

"Oh I almost forgot." She jumps up and turns to everyone. "How good are you all at swimming?" They all shrug.

"Alliyana?" Demetre looks confused.

"There is a cove a few miles away, where other vampires and mermaids meet!" she says excitedly and watches as the others smile and walk towards the water, clearly happy to find this cove.

Alliyana leads the way as she wades through the water and dives underneath. When she turns to see the others they are already swimming and are holding hands in twos so nobody becomes lost. She smiles and turns, swimming slower than usual so the others can keep up.

Forbidden Love

By the time Alliyana makes it to the cove a lot of the other mermaids are already relaxed and on the shore, Selia is standing looking very nervous and Alliyana gets the impression he has not told the others that she would be there. She is the first of the group to show herself by bringing her head above the surface.

"It's the princess!" shouts one of the mermaids and the rest begin to scramble, vampires standing to run away as mermaids look panicked at each other knowing its useless.

"Wait." Selia calls to them. "It's ok. She is just like us!" and every one stops, as they turn around looking wary they see her swim to them, surrounded vampire by heads appearing out of the water.

"He is right. I ask that accept us as part of this revolution. I too want this war over as do the rest of you. I do not wish to win or lose. I simply wish it to stop. I am in love with a vampire." She admits and the others gasp as Demetre comes to her side and throws his arm around her neck.

"What she said." He laughs and kisses her on the cheek. "OH Bread buns!" he swims to the shore and eyes the picnic baskets filled with bread.

"We welcome you princess." Says Selia.

"Yes, please join us!" Answers one of the others happily quickly followed with agreement from the others as they offer the baskets of bread around.

"We always bring to much food anyway." Says a female vampire chuckling.

"You are a servant?" Lillith asks stepping out of the water, her cheap maid clothes clinging to her womanly body. Water dripping from her hair and falling on her perfectly rounded breasts as she sways her hips walking towards the seated woman. Demetre watches as the other woman stops smiling and becomes entranced with the scene. He becomes excited as she swallows deeply and opens her mouth.

"I'm Lillith." She holds her hand out to introduce herself and the other woman takes it shakingly.

"I am Camille."

He goes back to Alliyana and points to the vampires so clearly lusting after one on another. "What do mermaids think of same sex relationships?" Alliyana's eyes widen and she grins mischievously.

"Actually, it's a very practised sexual experience for us."

"Oh baby I hit the jack pot!" he answers and dives on top of her kissing her deeply as they both fall into the water as Alliyana playfully tries to escape.

Chapter 10.

One of the vampires offers Alliyana a bread roll after she is done playing around with Demetre and she accepts graciously.

"That's a cheesy roll." Says the woman putting the basket back. "I'm Amber." She says sitting back down on the sand.

"Hello Amber. What does cheesy mean?" she holds the bread roll in front of her excited but also scared to taste the land food. "And what is bread?" Amber laughs at her light heartedly.

"Just try it. The others were the same to start with." She motions to the other mermaids in the sea.

Alliyana brings the bread roll to her mouth and takes a small bite, and instantly moans her appreciation as she savours the delicious taste.

"This is delicious! There isn't anything like this where we come from!" Amber smiles.

"It is nice to be able to share with you princess."

"Please call me Alliyana. Tonight I merely a friend." They both smile at each other as their new friendship is born when from behind them someone screams. When they both turn around they see a woman standing next to a tree, with dark skin, dark hair and dark eyes. Alliyana smiles in recognition.

"She walked out of the tree!" says one of the vampires backing away from her.

"Mut!" Alliyana calls and rises from the sea to greet the goddess. She hears the mumbles from the others as they aren't sure what to make of this. And another walks out from behind another tree that causes all the males to let their mouths hang open.

"Serapheena!" she welcomes as she stands before the two goddess's and bows before them, Demetre coming to her side after a moment.

"Is something wrong goddess's?" he asks worried as to why they would show themselves at the clearing.

"No Demetre." Says Mut. "We are here to give you all a gift. What you are going to experience will be hard on all of you, but we want you to know that we the greats don't only accept you all as you are but we thank you. We encourage you to go forth and make a new generation where love is love no matter who it is with!"

"I am Serapheena, goddess of love. And you are all accepted to me. I gave the gift of free will so you might love you wish. Now that is not the case and it saddens me. I ask you all to fight for freedom of love!" she shouts and everyone cheers.

Alliyana cries listening to these strangers that are willing to sacrifice all in order to let others find love with whoever they want to. The great mother steps forward, and she kisses Alliyana.

A tingling sensation spreads throughout her entire body, Alliyana doesn't even care how she managed to reach so high. A wave of happiness washes over her body as the goddess pulls away and everyone stares at her.

"Wow that's hot." Says Demetre as his eyes roam Alliyana's body. When she looks down Alliyana sees has a human body, but she is still covered with her tattoos. She looks at the goddess curiously.

"For one night only." She warns. "Make the most of it. And as for this…." She touches the vial Demetre had fastened around her when they met. "This was left by me, I had it hoped it would bring you two closer. Keep it with you. It will be very important at the end of this." She winks and walks toward another mermaid to kiss them. For one night they will be human. Alliyana stretches her muscles for minute before looking up to see Demetres eyes, intense and focused on only her.

She smiles and walks away from him, rubbing her hands across her new body as she goes, she screams and laughs when she turns and sees him running towards her. He lifts her up and walks briskly into the trees.

"You have quite a lot to answer for my darling." He smiles saucily at her and she shivers.

"I don't know what you mean." She states as he sets her down, back against a tree as he leans over and kisses her neck. Instantly she is pulling in a large shaky breath and moaning as his lips, tongue and teeth get to work on her new sensitive human skin.

"I wouldn't push me Alliyana, I'm bigger than you now!" he laughs at her and stands back to admire the view, pushing her long green hair back from her body as she sees him harden against the still wet material.

"I hardly think this is fair." She says and he smiles. Her hands reach out and rest on his hips, lifting up slightly and bring the flimsy wet shirt up towards his chest as he raises his arms allowing her to remove it and throw it away.

She stares at his chest feeling a rush between her legs at thought of him against her, the thought of him inside her. Her hands shake as the find the button on his trousers and slowly undo it, then slowly pull the zip down. The feel of her hand grazing lightly against his skin had his own breath coming faster and heavier, and he helped her to slide his jeans from his body and stepped out of them so he stood only in his boxer shorts. Which she also quickly discarded.

They stood staring for a moment, taking in each other's appearance and making a mental note for later. She made note of every muscle defined in his perfect stomach, the lines prominent showing they have been well used, the strength of his jaw line as he swallowed deeply, the powerful legs as he stood preparing to take her, and his lengthy erection which definatly stood to attention as he took in the way her patterns remained and danced across her breasts, he followed them down to her stomach which was perfectly shaped with wide hips and a little meat on her to look healthy, he followed them down her long sensual legs and his eyes fell on the hair-less triangle in the centre, where the swirling pattern increased for an elegant and beautiful site. He noticed her own hands moving, laying upon her own stomach as she bit her lower lip still staring at his erection. One moved up to just below her left breast as the other went to her neck.

Demetre took a step towards her, his own hands reaching to take her hips this time as he took her mouth, replacing her own teeth from biting her lip with his as she moaned at the sudden shock. He growled and pulled her close, hands moving from her hips to explore her body as he pushed her roughly against the tree trunk.

"Oh Goddess." She breathed.

"I don't want to hurt you." He whispered shakily. "But I'm about to lose control!"

"MMMM" was her only reply as his mouth found her breast, teeth and tongue teasing her nipple as she softly moaned in front of him. Her hand reached between them and took hold of his shaft as he growled again and her hand started to move up and down. His other hand reached down to her triangle and began to explore. His tongue thrust into her mouth sending a rush of excitement as she thought what else he could be thrusting inside her. She welcomed it and massaged it with hers allowing him to explore her with his fingers as he explored her with his tongue. Circling and entering her then circling again to tease her as she bucked her hips against his hand.

Her hand grabbing and twisting and pulling his large member in a rhythm made by the way his breathing increased rapidly to certain movements. She listened to his sounds as she moved her hand quickly then slowly and revelled in the thought of bringing this beautiful man before her to climax so intimately.

He wrenched himself away from her mouth crying "Oh fuck." Before pushing her harshly against the tree again, lifting her legs to wrap around him as he entered her then and there, the scream of pleasure coming from her as he sank deeper and deeper, forcing himself to wait a little while longer as his teeth sank into her neck.

He hadn't meant to draw blood, nor had he meant to leave bruises on her backside or breasts. But that was exactly how lost in the moment they both were. Her back arched as she looked up to the sky, his teeth and tongue sending her body crazy enough and as he penetrated her repeatedly becoming faster and harder and one of his hands raised to her breast she could feel her muscles tightening. She was building to climax with him on the edge already and as he thrust hard and fast one last time as deep as he could possibly go she released, screaming his name to the stars as his teeth clenched against her skin, agonising moans and growls coming from his throat as the throws of orgasm hit them both hard. They both collapse to the floor in a tangle of arms and legs, smiling and kissing as they try to catch their breath.

Chapter 11.

Lillith and Camille sat on the beach eating bread and talking. Sharing stories of the families they served and what they hope for from the war and it ending.

"I would like to find love." Said Lillith as she gushed, her wet clothes catching Camille's attention often as she would change position on the sand. "I mean obviously I am not a virgin. But... I have never felt love. Do you know what I mean?" she turned to face Camille and caught her staring at her breasts before she snapped her head to look away instantly seeming uncomfortable.

"Erm yeah I know what you mean. Well I have never found love either obviously and I'm not a virgin either, so yeah it would be nice to find love I suppose. Someone to cuddle with and spend time with and erm... other stuff." Camille was babbling and obviously nervous. Lillith raised up onto her knees and leant over to Camille, her long blonde hair cascading down to her ample cleavage, the wet clothes restricting the movement of her breasts as she breathed in and out. Though Camille was adamant they would bounce joyfully if she were to free them somehow. She tried to focus on the words Lillith was saying as she raised her thumb to her mouth and started biting at the nail nervously.

"What's your type?" Lillith had asked and Camille snapped out of her daze.

"Erm... round and firm. I mean, NO no erm I don't mean round and firm is my ... I ... well I mean I like... erm …." Lillith smiled and moved her hand to Camille's knee, still on her knees in front of her with her wet clothes that emphasized her curves alluringly.

"Good." She said before kissing Camille, after the immediate shock wore off Camille melted into the kiss. Hands going to pull Lillith down on top of her as she smiled inwardly reminding herself that even the goddess loved her and the others after all.

Lillith quickly removed her clothes and Camille was impressed, while her old fashioned clothes were scrubby and out dated her underwear was to be admired. Red and lacy panties matching the red lacy bra that barely held her beautiful breasts. She whistled at the site and laughed as Lillith started to pose for her on the beach.

"I think us vampires have been kept in the dark for far too long!" said Camille as Lillith crawled towards her on the sand, laughing as she pretended to growl like a cat stalking its prey.

Essy and Louissa were laid next to each other in a clearing in the centre of the island staring up at the clouds after their frivolous love making. Holding hands they pointed to all the different consolations they could find and started laughing as they started to make some of them up.

"Louissa, what did they do to you when they found out about us?" Asked Essy, thumb stroking the back of her lovers hand as she asked.

"It doesn't matter, it's done now." Came the reply after a silent minute. Essy sat up and looked her in the eye.

"It matters to me." She whispered. Louissa stared for a moment before also sitting up, only she let go of Essy's hand and turned away from her. "Please." She begged, placing her hand on Louissa's shoulder for comfort. Louissa's hand rested on top of Essy's and she leaned her cheek into it lovingly.

"They just sent me away love." She answered but her voice held a rough secret, and Essy knew she wasn't going to share it with her. She stood and walked around to sit in front of her, and taking both Louissa's hands in her own she kissed her lovingly.

"I love you Louissa, after this is over we will be together and no one can stand in our way." She knew it was pointless to apologise, this whole fight was because they shouldn't be ashamed of who they are so apologising for loving her would be useless. And untrue.

"I love you too Essy. I am just scared they will find you." The tears fall down Louissa's face as Essy reaches over to kiss them away.

"I have a feeling when this is over we need never be afraid again." She put Louissa's head on her shoulder and held her for a long while stroking the back of her head and mumbling words of comfort in between kissing her softly.

"Selia I don't get it, why does everyone seem happier to *come out* than us. Even here after being told its ok by the goddess!" Asks Droan, his fingers entwined with Selia's hair as he lays on his shoulder.

"I don't know I don't get it either. It just feels different." He agrees with his partner as they both ponder the reasoning's why the girls can openly admit they are gay and yet they can't.

"Maybe it's because you're scared ill fancy one of you!" Calls Demetre from behind them, they both shoot up not believing he had snuck up on them and heard, and their hearts pump wildly as Demetre just grins at them.

"Why are you spying on us?" Asks Droan.

"Hey don't hate me, at least you two guys are in love with someone of the same species!" Demetre chuckles.

"I heard that." Says Alliyana loudly as she stumbles out of the trees. "Sorry guys we went for a wander, honestly we only heard the last few minutes." She apologises feeling bad for interrupting their privacy. She turns and tries to pull Demetre away but he stands firm.

"Seriously though guys don't worry, even the humans are accepting this now and we are supposed to be way more advanced than them! Don't be afraid of who you are." He smiles at them and runs back into the trees yelling "Just as long as you know I'm off limits!" Laughing.

"Well that really depends..." shrugs Alliyana leaving the two men standing watching after them laughing slightly. They turn to face each other, Selia raises his hand to Droan who takes it and bows, and they both pretend to dance under the moonlight. Their hearts feeling lighter already now that somebody knows about them.

Demetre and Alliyana stop exploring as they reach a river, and Alliyana can't help but to slip in and sink to her neck, leaning her head against the edge of a tree. Demetre watches her with hungry eyes as she stares up at the sky.

"I can't believe we only met last night." She whispers.

"MMhmm." Comes his reply and she smiles, amused.

"So much has happened." She looks down at him as her eyes openly invite him to watch her. "I feel so... comfortable with you." Her voice takes on a seductive tone as he sits on the edge of the bank where the water meets the land, water crystal clear as she starts to touch her body, starting with her thighs.

"MMMM" he mumbles not really concentrating.

Her eyes burn into his as her hands move up her body and stroke her breasts, and he starts to harden again in his boxer shorts. He hadn't bothered to put his other clothes back on as they were soaking wet. Her hands skim up to her neck, then drag back down her body to her thighs again brushing her nipples as they made their way firmly over her breasts.

Her tongue licks at her lips as she brings her hands up and down her body again, for some reason this sweeping motion sends Demetres body into a frenzy and he moans out loud, standing frozen with desire as his erection threatens to explode out the tight confines of his shorts.

She takes a deep breath, her chest filling and making her nipples stick slightly out of the water as her hands gather between her legs. She softly strokes herself, glorying in the burning desire radiating from Demetre as he watches her. This normally private act of masturbation made so much better by the excitement of him watching her. She moans quietly as her mouth opens, she sees the look of desperation on Demetres face almost as though the only thing he wants in the world is to witness her bring herself to climax. As she starts to stroke harder and faster at the swelling bud between her legs Demetre removes himself from his boxers. Alliyana's eyes widen as she sees the size of him, and he grabs the pulsating erection as he watches her, awkwardly turning to sit so his legs dangle into the water, she cries out with pleasure as she watches. Both of them getting off on watching the other pleasure themselves as they work themselves to orgasm, Alliyana is the first of the two to be sent into convulsions. Her head turning one way then the next furiously as her eyes close tightly. Her fingers working vigorously before they are replaced with Demetres hard quivering member, he thrusts deep inside her calling out loudly as he moans and groans already so close. She bucks her hips closer to his desperate for a deeper penetration as her legs wrap around him, his hands finding her nipples as they both explode in a shower of pleasure, waves crashing of pleasure over the both of them as she cries his name and holds him close, fingers digging into his flash as her release eases and her body relaxes.

He kisses her shoulder, her cheek, her forehead, anything he can find of hers close to his face he kisses it. Sweat dripping from him as he tries to control his breathing between kisses.

"I love you Alliyana." He whispers to her. "I love you so much." When she raises his head to look into his eyes she sees tears brimming, and she understands. She has waited a long time to feel this way as well.

"I love you to Demetre." And she kisses him again.

While the vampires and mermaids are all enjoying their night off from responsibility; gifted to them by the goddess's, no one is aware of the eyes watching them all. Jullian takes in the disgusting scenes in outrage, and after watching the princess make love to vile vampire he immediately makes up his mind in his next move. He turns quickly and swims to Miaya in search of the queen, sure she will want to know what the vampires are doing to her precious daughter.

Susan Hatton

Chapter 12.

Alliyana wakens to the seagulls squawking, she is laid with her head on Demetres stomach with the soft flow of water on her legs. She raises her hand to see human fingers still there and hears a whisper of the goddess's voice on the wind.

"Yes my dear, you have time for one more." The chuckling voice tells her, and she looks up to Demetre as he sleeps. Vampires don't need much sleep at all, and in their shaded spot under the trees he should be fine against the sun for a few hours at least. She pulls herself up and throws one leg over his naked body, his boxers hanging from a tree branch close by to dry.

He moves a little and opens his eyes to see Alliyana sitting on top of him with playful eyes.

"Darling you have no idea what you are dealing with." He mumbles debating whether or not to get into the *morning glory* talk.

"We have time for one more go the goddess says." His smile broadens and his hands find her hips.

"Is that so? Well then how about we make it worth it!" he lifts her off him and rolls out from under her, she stands up looking confused. He takes her hips again and moves her to a tree branch low enough for her to sit on, and he kneels in front of her. He spreads her legs and puts his hands on her thighs before kissing her knees. Her arms go behind her back to steady her as his fingertips knead and massage her soft flesh. His kisses trail from her knees up, his tongue following the patterns of her skin to the very top as he brushes his lips over her opening. She sucks air in as she grits her teeth against the urge to cry out.

"Does that feel good?" he asks ruggedly, his hot breath making her squirm as she watches him envelope her clitoris within his mouth. Her mouth forms the shape of an O as her entire body stiffens. The pleasure is so intense it borders on unbearable and she goes from stiff as a board to limbs flailing around within seconds, her hand finds the top of his head and grabs his hair. She cries out for him to stop but he doesn't, he knows if he stopped she would be disappointed. He keeps going caressing her sensitive spot with his tongue while his fingers work inside her to bring to an agonising and powerful, and extremely wet climax as she moans repeatedly and cries his name.

"Fuck." Say's Demetre as he looks up at her when he is finished, hands still kneading the flesh of her thighs as he breaths deeper. "Just hearing you finish is enough to send any man over the edge!"

Alliyana stands and pushes him onto his back on the floor, about to take control and let him have his finished when a splashing sound distracts her. She looks up to see the scolding eyes of her mother as she raises from the water to see what Alliyana is doing. A smiling Jullian right behind her.

"Mother." She says unbelievingly.

"Not quite." Says Demetre confused, when he looks in the direction Alliyana is staring he jumps up.

"Well here we go I guess." He says standing.

The sky darkens and thunder crashes above them.

"Alliyana." Her mother calls. "It is time to come back now. We have much to discuss." Her mother orders to which Alliyana stands. But she does not walk anywhere.

"No. I will not go with you mother." She replies and her mother sighs.

"You see my queen? The vampire has be-spelled her somehow. She knows not what she says." Jullian is at her mother's side feeding her the poison she needs to hear, twisting her mind against her own daughter to get what he wants.

"There is only the magic of the goddess's here!" Shouts Alliyana.

"Yes. And who the hell are you slime ball?" Yells Demetre to Jullian.

"I am Alliyana's Fiancé!" he replies angrily and Demetre laughs.

"Oh dear, so this could be awkward then!" He shouts as he puts his arm around Alliyana's waist and pulls her close, watching with an evil smile as Jullian's eyes narrow and his mouth pulls tight in anger. "Gonna cry slime ball?" asks Demetre.

"Why not find a woman of your own species to violate, or are you sick of vampires too!" he spits.

"I find vampires very alluring actually." States Alliyana.

"Nor me." Says another mermaid in human form, walking from the trees as many more join them.

Alliya gasps as she looks at everyone. "Alliyana what have you done?"

"I have found love mother, I wish could find it too!" she snaps.

"This ends now!" shouts her mother, and at a wave of her hand all the mermaids are turned back into mermaid form. "Return to Miaya this instant!" she thrusts her arm down aggressively and without warning, the mermaids are forced from the land and into the sea.

Alliyana feels the pull, and it carries her half way down the beach before she tries to stop it. She forces herself to try to fight against her mother's power and as a result is stuck, pulling herself forward so to be with Demetre.

"No!" he screams and runs to help her, but Aliya sends him flying back along with the other vampires.

Forbidden Love

"Mother stop!" Cries Alliyana not sure she can hold on much longer. "Please Mut, help me!" the tears fall down her face as she starts to think she can't do this.

Time suddenly seems to slow down as Alliyana lowers her face about to give up, and she rises from her body almost like a ghost.

"What is this?" she asks scared.

"I am here for you child. I understand how hard this is, so I thought you could use a moment." Mut stands behind Alliyana on the beach and puts her hand on her shoulder while they both take in the scene before them. Demetres face is etched with worry as he is crying out to her, the other vampires look terrified yet they still fight on, Alliyana looks like some grotesque creature crawling the beach as her mother pulls her back and she sees why the goddess is showing this to her.

"When did my mother become this?" She asks as she turns to face her. Her eyes close and she collapses when she sees the look on her mother's face. The paranoid anger of her daughter betraying her, the wretched influence Jullian as he whispers in her ear, the lack of love or care as she uses her powers to force her own daughter against her will. "That woman is not my mother." She whispers and Mut nods sombrely.

"It is true child. But please understand before you decide to hate her. Imagine your love for Demetre, think of the horror you feel towards your own mother for trying to keep you apart. Her love was stolen by Demetres father, and not only did she have her love stolen she was then thrust into the role of queen without a king. She was never able to mourn her loss. She lost herself to bitterness and resentment." Alliyana puts her head in her hands and cries at the goddess's words torn between hating her mother and feeling sorry for her. She realises that the only hate she feels is because her mother is stopping her from being with Demetre.

"You know what you have to do child." The goddess says to her and Alliyana cries harder. "If your mother dies, you become the new ruler. Married or not. You can set the new laws, you can change what she destroyed, and you can set your mother free from her prison of hatred."

"How can you ask this of me!" she cries angrily. "How can you show yourself and pretend to care." She spits toward the goddess who sheds a tear at Alliyana's words.

"I know child. It is more than anyone should ask. This is cruel. And it breaks my heart as well as yours." The goddess looks straight into her eyes as she cries more, her pain bared to Alliyana.

"It cannot be done." Says Alliyana and turns from the goddess.

"If that is your true answer then I accept it child." Alliyana stops and turns back to stare at her. "But know that if this be the way it goes, nothing will change. You will be forced back to Miaya, where you will be forced to marry Jullian." The goddess points to him. She takes a deep breath as though her next words are too painful to speak out loud. "He will beat you and rape you, and many more soldiers will die as he becomes overwhelmed with power and greed. He will fixate only on winning this war and then starting many others. You do have a choice child, I am simply telling you the outcome of each." And she looks towards Demetre with a small smile, not needing words to tell Alliyana that Demetre as her king would do a much better job, as he now risks himself to protect her.

"But how?" she whispers.

"You know how powerful you are Alliyana. You have never unleashed it but you know. Your power is vast and it is high time you used it. I love you Alliyana, and so does your mother. Deep down past the hate she loves you. Now you must set that love free." The goddess kisses her forehead and turns to walk away as Alliyana is sucked back into reality.

Caught momentarily off guard her mother succeeds in pulling her back towards the sea for a few feet.

"No." Alliyana says out loud as she stops in the air. She stands and turns to face her mother, eyes and patterns glowing as she accepts her power. "I will not return with you mother." She raises from the floor and hovers. Opening and closing her hand slightly she sets up a powerful barrier around the vampires still on the land, it stops her mother using her power against them but it also stops them coming near her.

"You dare to challenge the queen of the sea? Why I do believe it is time you taught your daughter a less..." Jullian says, but before he finishes his sentence Alliyana flicks her hand towards him, and a wave crashes into his body. It sends him flying miles and miles away as the water starts to whirl and crash beneath her, it rises to caress her skin and welcome her. It comforts her.

"Alliyana do not push me." Her mother warns with a dangerous edge to her voice.

Chapter 13.

Alliyana brings her hands together harshly, and the sea obeys her command. It sends large aggressive waves crashing into her mother from both directions. Alliya only just defers the attack in time. She stares at her daughter as it becomes clear that she is going to fight this to the end.

"You are prepared to die for him?" she asks her daughter as the thought disgusts her. "You embarrass me."

"I would die a thousand times for him and the others!" Alliyana answers her mother with pride.

Alliya spits on the ground in disgust. "You are no daughter of mine!" she says harshly but Alliyana just laughs.

"We agree on something at least then!"

"How dare you?" her mother asks. "I brought you up, I fed you, and I tried to do right by you."

"No you didn't mother. You brought man after man into our home, into your bed, to fill the emptiness you felt when father died. You stopped me from talking about him as though to remember him was a sin, you stopped coming into my room when I woke crying from night mares, you shouted from the hall for me to go back to sleep, you couldn't even comfort your own daughter you were so twisted. Everything I did was wrong and you didn't want to know my opinions or views, if what I did didn't meet your standards it wasn't good enough. You didn't bring me up mother you dragged me up!"

Her mother looked hurt, as though she knew her daughters words were true and was suddenly regretful. Alliyana hoped it was an opening, she hoped it was a chance to make her mother see the truth.

"Step down graciously mother. There doesn't have to be a fight we can talk about this. We can be the way we used to be when one of us talked and the other listened. We could both walk away from this. I don't want to have to hurt you." She says quietly but her voice booms through the sky, in the back of her mind Alliyana registers the voice of the vampires as they shout to be freed and help her. Demetre screams her name terrified she is on a suicide mission yet powerless to escape the bubble of protection.

"You think you can take me on? I gave birth to you!" Alliya shouts raising her hands to have the sea deny her command, telling Alliyana that her command had been to cause death.

"No! Even the sea has turned against *you*. My mother gave birth to me, the woman who laughed as my father read to me, the woman who kissed me goodnight every night, the woman who sang with me and played with me and spoke to me and made time for me, *she* gave birth to me. You just took over her body when my father died. The sea won't answer to you anymore because it does not recognise you."

"You will not speak of your father! That coward left us when we needed him, it was his own fault he died going to war with the soldiers anyway he should have stayed home with us."

"My father was a hero! He put himself at risk just like the soldiers did and it was brave of him. He led his soldiers instead of telling them what to do. My father was not afraid of anything!"

"Your father was a fool, an imbecile!"

Her words sliced through Alliyana like a knife, she felt the pain deep in her heart and switched to autopilot to escape the agonising truth that her mother had said those words freely and meant them. Her mother really did think of her father as a coward, and that brought so much dishonour to his memory she felt the tears well up inside of her just thinking about it. But her mother wasn't done.

"He didn't have an ounce of courage or sense and I see you fall into the same category. Stupid and foolish. Chasing around with vampires and letting cloud your silly little mind. I should kill him slowly for what he has done to you."

Alliyana hadn't known what she had done until after she had done it, the magnificent wave that crashed into her mother had sent her soaring violently into the trees on the island. Alliyana had screamed. She felt instantly ashamed. She lowered herself to the floor and started running, crying for her mother. The bubble holding the vampires must have stopped too, as she heard the foot steps behind her and

Demetre calling to her. Begging her not go in there alone. She hit the trees and darted between branches and tree stumps calling her mother's name, tears flowed freely down her face. Her feet were being sliced to ribbons by stones and pebbles and twigs but she kept running without feeling a thing. Demetre trailed behind trying desperately to keep up with her.

She felt her presence before she saw her, Mut was stood with her back to Alliyana and as she turned she saw her mother. She had been impaled by a tree branch, her body still as her eyes stared out into the trees opposite her.

"NOOO!" Alliyana cried as she collapsed to the floor, she barely noticed Demetres arms engulfing her as he held her and rocked her. The goddess held her head low, her own tears spilling from her face and crashing to the floor at the sad events that the day had brought. To think a woman could have been so twisted by bitterness that she had had to be killed by her own daughter to save the many who depended on her.

"Holy fuck." Demetre had said after holding her for a few seconds, and he stood in front of her. When Alliyana raised her head she saw the most beautiful site she had ever seen. Her mother stood in front of her, tears of joy in her eyes and her arms open to her daughter as she sank to her knees and held her. Alliyana aw the body still hanging from the tree, the face all disgruntled and lifeless eyes had her cringing. Her mother's spirit turned her to face her again.

"Thank you Alliyana, do not worry about that." She nudged her head towards her final resting place and smiled. "It is not me, that is hatred and anger. It is the prison you rescued me from daughter. And I am so proud of you." Her mother chocked on the tears as she embraced her daughter again. Kissing her forehead and rubbing her back. "I am so proud of you, I love you Alliyana please forgive me for what I have done. I have wronged you, you should have never had to do that. I can't believe how strong you are child." The tears flowed from everyone in the clearing, and as Alliya stood she looked to Demetre, and she lowered her head in shame.

"You do not need my blessing, nor do I deserve to give it. But I want you to know that should you ask, it would be yours. You have saved my daughter. And for that I owe you my heart. Take care of her vampire, and stop this hatred and war!"

"Alliya I don't know what to say." He answers. "I accept your blessing a hundred times, and I don't think I'll be allowed to look after her but if it's any consolation I feel safe!" he whispers to her making her laugh.

"You are right, she does not need taking care of."

A man steps from a tree to their right, and he looks around the small group with a smile from ear to ear.

"Father?" Alliyana asks in disbelief.

"Daughter!" he yells and he throws his arms around her crying to the heavens. "Oh Alliyana my sweet sweet girl I missed you! Oh I am so proud of the queen you have grown to be. And you are now queen." He reminds her. He looks over to Demetre who instantly remembers it is his father that caused his death, and he hangs his head in shame.

"You vampire! If not for you my daughter wouldn't know love, she would not have had the courage to fight, my wife would still be tortured and my kingdom in peril. I owe you a great deal. I give you my blessing, as I don't really have much on me right now." This time Demetre laughs and he kisses Alliyana.

"We must be going now." Says Mut nodding to Alliyana's parents. "Androwda, Alliya, say your final goodbyes. I'll give you a few minutes." And she steps through the tree bark and back within nature.

"She will come back to you two when we are done." Says Androwda as he takes his daughter in his arms again. "Alliyana I am proud of you and I love you, and you will be the best queen Miaya has ever known because of this experience. Demetre I am proud of you as well. I am proud to call you my son in law." He hold his hand on Demetres shoulder as a sign of respect, and Demetre clasps it firmly within his right hand.

"I am proud of you both, I owe you both everything and I am so proud of the pair of you. And Alliyana, your right. Your father is a hero." She bursts into tears as does Alliyana and they embrace each other again.

Alliyana's parents follow the goddess into the tree bark to go on their adventure into the next realm together, and Mut returns in their place. Out from another tree steps Serapheena. Who takes one look at her surroundings and throws her hands together.

"Well there is a gift to sort out for you both buuuut I think we should maybe move the party somewhere else, don't you?" she clicks her fingers together and they find themselves in the dining area of a great hall, marble steps and pillars everywhere with intricate gold patterns everywhere.

"Where are we?" asks Demetre and Serapheena raises an eyebrow smiling mischievously.

"The land of the greats, of course." She answers as both women and men rush over to her, brushing her long red hair and removing the long white material from her body before replacing with a long green piece and clasping it at one shoulder.

"But we are not great. We are not allowed here." Answers Alliyana confused as one of the woman start to brush her hair and she can't bring herself to tell her no as the brush on her scalp feels so relaxing.

"Do you want to tell them, or shall I?" She asks Mut.

Susan Hatton

Chapter 14.

"I shall let you take the pleasure." Answers Mut smiling just as mischievously as Serapheena.

"Well, all of us greats owe you both a great gift for what you have done and still have to do. The worst is over, but there is still a long way to go. You are going to have to change the way these mermaids and vampires have been taught before they accept you. We think we have come up with the most perfect idea to both help with your task ahead and reward you both." Serapheena closes her eyes and opens her arms, as does Mut. They are quickly joined with a few other men and women they assume must be other gods.

Alliyana Notices a strange feeling in her arms and legs, and she closes her eyes as a wave nausea takes over her body. She reaches out for Demetre but she can't feel him, opening her eyes a little she sees a blur sitting on the floor beside her and she quickly joins him on the floor.

"What's going on?" Demetre roars, voice full of panic as he tries to stand.

"Shit I probably should have warned them first." They heard Serapheenas voice before their vision cleared. "Here come sit and have a drink."

They feel arms supporting them and leading them to seats, and the take the drinks offered to them as the waves of dizziness begin to decrease. Alliyana throws her back and takes a deep steadying breath. Then another. Then she looks at Serapheena.

"What the hell was that?" she asks. Serapheena smiles widely.

"Come take a look." She walks Alliyana to a mirror and Alliyana almost faints. She has the body of a human, but all her patterns have remained. She moves the material draped over her body when arriving and see's what Demetre saw when she was turned human for the night on the island.

"But I am supposed to be queen of the ocean." She says confused, she turns at the sound of Demetre groaning and she is struck with the most amazing and beautiful site of all.

Demetre stands from his seat, with white material draped around his waist which he quickly discards. He stands tall and turns to see Alliyana. The patterns on his face stop her in her tracks. He has a human body, but mermaid patterns covering his face, arms and legs. They are masculine and rugged and work to make his entire body look even more chiselled.

As he takes in the site of her before him with her human bodies and mermaid patterns, part of his mind tries to figure out what is going on but most of it is saying "God she looks hot!"

"You better kiss him sweetness, or I'm going to!" Serapheena whispers and she laughs despite herself, then shakes her head.

"Wait, what the hell is going on?" she asks again and Serapheena smiles nodding to Mut to explain. "How can I be human when I have to rule the ocean?"

"You are not human Alliyana, you are a great. You and Demetre now rule the sky and the sea." She says to them both and they look at each other in shock.

"So I am a god?" Demetre asks puzzled.

"You sure are!" She beams looking from one to the other.

"Can I still wear jeans?" he asks and Alliyana laughs out loud at the serious look on his face.

"Click your fingers and think of what you want." Serapheena says huskily making his eyes widen.

"Do it fast, I think Serapheena might be struggling to control herself." Alliyana laughs as Serapheena stares at Demetres new god like body, biting her lip. She looks at Alliyana smiling knowingly.

"I can't help it, I'm the goddess of love!" She replies. "If it helps at all I could remove your gown and stare at you instead." Alliyana knows she speaks the truth. The goddess of love is bisexual, she has to be to love everyone.

Demetre snaps his fingers and is suddenly clothed in jeans and a short. He smiles and clicks his fingers and Alliyana is suddenly dressed in black matching bra and panties with stockings to her thighs and high heels on her feet.

Serapheena voices her approval as she sits herself down, getting comfortable for the show. Alliyana stands up straight and looks straight at Demetre with a stern expression.

"Yeah baby." He yells and clicks his fingers again, suddenly she has teacher style glasses and a long rule in her hands. This time she can't help but laugh at him, as do Mut and Serapheena.

"He has good taste though." Serapheena nods approvingly. Alliyana clicks her fingers and is covered with the same white material from before.

"So where do we go from here then?" she asks as the laughter stops and things become serious again.

"You will win over the mermaids before you win over the vampires, so I suggest you go to Demetres parents and at least make a start. Tell them who you are and what you have done, and also what you have become. And remember, you are now a goddess Alliyana as well as a queen. Nobody can harm you." Mut kisses her cheek and then Demetres cheek.

"I won't kiss either of you, or I won't let you go." Serapheena winks at them. "There's just something about fresh gods and goddess, so dam hot!" Demetre points at her.

"You're a vixen!" he accuses and she winks at him, pouting.

"Should I be worried about you two?" Alliyana laughs, instantly realising that she isn't nor has she been worried about them in the slightest. Serapheena is a goddess, the goddess of love! And Demetre is a stud, and she never doubted him for a minute even though they are both serial flirts.

"I love you." She says to him seriously, in that moment grateful for what she has and what she has experienced.

"I love you Alliyana." And as she throws her arms around him she unleashes the tears that had been waiting for the last few days, she cried and cried and they sank to the floor and cried together.

Mut and Serapheena had understood completely and ordered that they be left alone. They had suffered immense amounts and it was extremely unfair especially on Alliyana, and Demetre held her while she cried all the way wishing he could do more to help ease her pain than stroke her hair. Her tears and sobbed had his own eyes brimming as he fought desperately to stay strong for her. When she pulled away from him finally drying her eyes he had clicked his fingers, and a meal with wine had appeared before them.

"Eat Darling, you are going to need your strength. We aren't finished yet." And while they both ate some food and drank some wine in the great hall still with only a very slight clue of what was happening, Mut and Serapheena praised the two landers for their courage to the other greats. And the story was told.

Susan Hatton

Chapter 15.

Alliyana and Demetre stop outside of his parents' house, and Demetre looks to her for comfort. He really doesn't want to go in there, and he *really* doesn't want to take Alliyana in there. She smiles warmly to him and holds his hand.

"Come on God of the sky and sea." She teases him. "What are you afraid of?" winking as she leads him to the door and pushes him in front. It is his parents' home, he must open the door and enter first. He walks over the threshold and breaths deeply, instantly regretting it as his nostrils fill with the old musky smell of dirt and grime.

"Is that you Demetre? We are in the dining hall, your father is here tonight so you may grovel to him for forgiveness too." He follows the sound slowly to the dining hall and pulls Alliyana behind him. When he enters he sees his mother and father reading at the table, and the twins are there. They instantly stare up at him and look confused before smiling at each other.

"Who's she? And what's happened?" The twins say excitedly together and Demetres parents snap their heads up to see what they are talking about, their jaws landing on the floor as they both stand up in shock. Alliyana laughs as the twins stand and rush over to shake her hand.

"My name is Brianna." Smiles one widely.

"And I'm Imaara." Says the other. "Are you our brother's girlfriend?"

"Girls!" their mother demanded, but they ignored her. Demetre laughed and bent to cuddle them both.

"Now girls don't go embarrassing me!" he said pleading with them. They looked at each other and then turned to Alliyana.

"Well? Are you his girlfriend?" she coughs awkwardly.

"I suppose you could say that." Brianna and Imaara laugh and make 'ohhh' sounds at Demetre singing 'Demetres got a girlfriend!' while pretending to kiss him. Alliyana laughs out loud at the girls and they both stop but continue smiling.

"Girls come over here now!" Their mother orders. Brianna looks back at her with a face that just looks bored. They both look at Alliyana then turn to Demetre.

"We like her. Keep her." They say in unison and skip over to their mother, ignoring her arms spread to accept them and walking around her to sit on the carpet.

"What is this?" Asks Demetres father.

Dracula stands tall and wiry with jet black hair, his features look almost non-existent he is so thin. He raises his arm and points one bony finger to Demetre.

"Come here boy. Tell this silly thing to leave my house and come tell me you wish forgiveness. I won't always be so kind as to give it!" he says harshly, words dripping menace as he gives Alliyana a look of disgust that she returns with a grin and a wave.

"Who are you?" demands Demetres mother. Alliyana steps forward and raises her chin.

"I am the daughter of the king your husband murdered. Do pardon my intrusion on your lives here tonight. It is only that we have come to take over the war." Alliyana states as calm as though she were reeling off a shopping list!

Dracula and Driana stare open mouthed as the girls turn to watch excitedly, almost as though waiting for this woman to get her revenge.

"She is Alliyana, daughter of Androwda and Alliya who have both tonight given us their blessings, as has the goddess Mut and the goddess Serapheena. And much more has happened too." He opens his arm to Alliyana who smiles lovingly at him and walks into his embrace. "We are no god and goddess of the sky and the sea. And I am telling you this war is over." Demetre says boldly to his parents who just continue to stare. The girls are open mouthed and bright eyed in awe and Alliyana waves to them, they eagerly start bouncing up and down and grinning but Driana stands in front of them.

"You do not acknowledge my girls you filthy creature, I don't know how you have managed to bespell my son but I will not let you harm them!"

"Why mother, so you can palm them off to the highest bidder? Pretend to love them until they go against YOUR ways and then banish them? I think not! I say it again." The air in this little dining room becomes thick and dense, and they hear lightning boom outside. When Alliyana looks at Demetre she see his eyes glowing red as well as the patterns on his skin, his parents shrink back in fear. "The war is over, send everyone home. From here on there are no rules. You will accept everyone you come into contact with. Whomever they are! And you will accept your new daughter in law with only kind words to others. And you will accept that you her your lives. Had she not been here today I doubt I could have contained myself." His parents get down on their knees grovelling for their lives, the girls behind them rolling their eyes as they stand run towards Alliyana. They ignore Demetre and take both Alliyana's hands as they lead her from the room.

"You can't leave children with them, they are insane!" Says Brianna.

"Do you agree Imaara?" she asks the other and he smiles shocked.

"How did you know I am Imaara? No one ever tells us apart not even them!" she gestures back to her parents.

"Well when you introduced yourself to me as Imaara I remembered the only difference between you two. You have a freckle on your cheek." She touched the freckle with her finger lightly and the girls both smiled, turned to Demetre and said "She stays!" in unison as they grabbed her hands again.

"Do you know what? I think I have the perfect place for these girls!" says Demetre as he clicks his fingers.

Forbidden Love

They appear on the island where the vampires were now talking with the mermaids who made it back to the island. When they see Alliyana and Demetre they all turn and run, but they stop when they notice Alliyana's human appearance and Demetres patterns. Demetre smiles widely and clicks his fingers, houses appear on the island and the others recoil in shock. Turning back to Demetre and Alliyana they all bow their heads in respect of the new god and goddess.

"No!" Alliyana shouts and everyone looks up confused. She grabs Demetres hand runs toward them, he knows instantly what she plans to do. She stops a short distance away, and sweepingly bows low to show her respect to these mermaids and vampires.

"Alliyana we didn't even do anything!" Says Essy as though she is angry.

"You were here!" Alliyana cries and hugs her. "That is more than others, you all gave me more than our own parents could!" she gestures her hands around them small group.

Demetre takes Brianna and Imaara by their hands and leads them to the group.

"Lillith!" they squeal and run to her, and Lillith bursts into happy tears when she sees the girls. She looks up at Demetre who just shrugs.

"They need somewhere to stay and someone to look after them." she nods, accepting the girls as her own. She had loved them as soon as they were born, as did Demetre. But he had other godly things to be doing these days. Like a sea goddess. He raised his brows and smiled mischievously at Alliyana, who returned his grin with challenge in her eyes.

Just before the others witnessed them both disappear they heard him growl and click his fingers.

The end.

Epilogue.

Demetre stepped into the large marble bathroom, Alliyana was in the shower and he leant himself against the counter as he took in the view through the clear glass shower doors.

Water cascaded from head to toe emphasizing her curves as it ran down the smoothness of her body and ripped from her sumptuous buttocks. He watched mesmerised as her expert hands lathered soap all over her body, paying extra care to her breasts as he moaned softly from inside the shower. The sound bounced off the tile walls all around him and Demetre was struck with an urge so intense he growled as he lunged forward and entered the shower, clicking his fingers remove his clothes.

She had heard him enter and knew he watched, she played with her nipples remembering the time they masturbated together by the river and how sensual it had been. She remembered how it had felt to watch him lick his lips while watching her. And now she felt his hardness brush against her back as his hands came around to find her wrists, he pulled her hands away from her breasts and placed them on the cold tiled wall of the bathroom. Grabbing her hips he positioned himself ready to enter and she started to move her hips slightly, desperate to have the feel of him. He waited, torturing her and himself but desperately waiting for those words from her mouth.

"Oh god please!" she cried and Demetre smiled to himself.

"This god will grant your wish." He slams into her as she cries out in instant orgasm, one hand on her breast and on her hip as he breathed rugged and harshly, penetrating deeper and deeper as he built her to climax and she screamed his name. He caught her as her legs collapsed and withdrew himself. Clicking his fingers they were dry and in the bedroom, and he began laying her down on her back as he positioned her feet on his chest.

"Oh my god!" she cried as he entered her, his tip running over special spot he had discovered that made her spasm and cry out more and more. He thrust into her paying extra attention to that spot inside as his hand came around and he started to tease her clitoris. Her leg muscle contracting as the waves of pleasure passed through her body, even her toes threatening to cramp if she clenched them anymore.

"Oh god, Demetre stop! Oh god, OH GOD!" the thing she enjoyed the most was being able to say stop and he wouldn't. She knew if he stopped when she begged him to she would be left wanting more. *Needing* more. The pleasure waves became much more intense and she had to grit her teeth against the tightening's in her body as he thrust harder and deeper. Her feet moved and her ankles crossed behind his back as his mouth came crashing down and their lips found each other, pumping faster he took her bottom lip between his teeth and growled, plunging himself as deep as he could as he released his seed. She screamed his name to the ceiling as they both collapsed in a tangle on the bed.

"What would you like do next on our honeymoon, Goddess?" he asks her with a husky voice and raised eye brow.

"I think…. Sex. For a change I mean." She laughs and he looks disgusted.

"I'm not a piece of meat you know!" He pretends to be upset.

"Oh really? Maybe I married the wrong god!" Alliyana replies, and she smiles widely as Demetre growls in his throat at her.

"I love the way you growl. Pure animalistic lust!" she says as he dives on her and she giggles, playfully trying to get away as he nibbles on her neck and bare breasts.

Made in the USA
Charleston, SC
20 June 2014